# SADIE
# (A Fairy's Tale)

C M Williams

Illustrated by
Alece Ashley

authorHOUSE®

AuthorHouse™ LLC
1663 Liberty Drive
Bloomington, IN 47403
www.authorhouse.com
Phone: 1-800-839-8640

Published by AuthorHouse  03/19/2014

ISBN:     978-1-4918-7233-8 (sc)
          978-1-4918-7234-5 (e)

Library of Congress Control Number: 2014902397

## For my grandchildren

*Mercedes (my Sadie),*
*Marcus (my Bohdi),*
*Daman (my Finn) and*
*Anthony (my Asher)*

*You inspire me.*
*I love you all.*


*To my daughter Alece:*
*Thank you for all*
*your love and encouragement.*
*Without it this book would*
*not have been possible.*


*To my husband (Papa):*
*Thank you for believing in me.*

Whispering in hushed tones, the two women move farther away from the bed where their captive lies magically bound. He struggles against his bonds when their backs are turned, always keeping a close eye on the two. His eyes glitter with hatred.

"You must do it now," the princess pleads. "I do not know how long the bonds I've placed on him will hold."

"I cannot!" her friend says, horrified by the request. "What if you are wrong about him?"

"I am not wrong!" she hisses. "You must do this. It is the only way to save him! Listen to me: If you do not stab him in the heart soon, the madness will take a stronger hold on him. It will continue to darken his soul until he is lost to us forever. Please! You must hurry!"

Walking to the edge of the bed, her friend stands beside it and gazes down at the man lying in it. Looking deep into his eyes, she searches for something, anything that will tell her that all she has been told about him is true.

Glacial blue eyes stare back at her, pleading, "Do not do this. She is wrong. Look at me. I am well. I know you, and I know that you would not want me to die by your hand. Release me and all will be forgotten."

"Do not listen to him!" she snaps. "Do it! He is only stalling for more time to find a way to free himself. Do it now! I command you!"

Lifting her ice dagger above her head she hesitates. Cold eyes stare up at her and he begins to struggle, bucking and twisting, pulling against his bonds. "Do not do this!" he commands through clenched teeth. Hatred flashes in the depths of his eyes, but only for an instant and then it's gone, replaced once again by his pleading stare.

"Do it! Do it now!" the princess shouts.

Convinced after what she saw in the depths of his eyes, she plunges her dagger deep into his chest, piercing his heart, and then withdraws it quickly.

His cry breaks the silence in the room, the sound more animal than man, more from hatred than pain. He roars, cursing them both at the top of his lungs, hatred glittering in the depths of his eyes as he struggles in earnest against his bonds.

The ice slowly spreads through his heart, his struggles slowing until finally they cease altogether as his eyes flutter closed. When he finally rests peacefully in a deep, deathlike slumber, the two women gaze down upon the beautiful golden man. Pain and sorrow etched into their lovely faces, their tears flowing freely.

# DREAMS

She waits, hovering in a dark corner of the room. Ancient and all-powerful, the angelic creature smiles, her periwinkle eyes sparkling with delight, her long golden hair and white robes floating softly around her. Knowing that the child finally slumbers, she approaches the small form snuggled deep within the covers of her bed. Reaching down to brush a few strands of golden hair from the child's face, she smiles once again, twirling the soft strands around a finger. She allows herself a moment to savor the feel of them as they slip from her hand, strands of hair exactly like her own. She lovingly caresses the child's soft cheek as she whispers,

*"In your dreams we can play.*
*In your dreams we must stay"*

While sleeping, the young girl begins to dream of lying on a white sandy beach beneath a brilliant blue sky. Reclining on a soft fluffy chaise, she looks out across the crystal blue ocean, familiar yet alien. The waves roll and sparkle in a rhythmic pattern designed to soothe and relax before curling and crashing into the shore.

Lazily, the girl twirls and digs her toes in the soft, warm sand and raises her arms above her head, enjoying the feel of the sun's warm rays. Feeling peaceful and happy, she looks over at the radiant woman lying beside her. In her dream she has known this woman all her life as her grandmother. Beautiful and golden, the woman smiles warmly at her and says, "So tell me all about this school that you and your friends attend. I want to know everything!"

Stretched out beneath a brilliant azure sky, the two of them lapse into comfortable conversation. They only get to see each other once a year, so they try to make the most of it. They spend their days talking while bobbing up and down, relaxing in the swells of the ocean. They take long leisurely walks on the beach hunting for shells as the sun slowly slips below the horizon. They feast on the most wonderful-tasting food, which the young girl only gets to eat while visiting her grandmother.

Slowly the fog of sleep begins to fade, and a nose peaks out from under the covers. Warm and cozy, the remnants of her dream still lingering, she sniffs the air to discover the smell of pancakes and bacon greeting her senses. Her eyes pop open, her brain remembering, and throwing back the covers she kicks them down with her feet and stretches for just a minute. She then sits up and looks around, the familiar room that she hasn't slept in since last year bringing a smile to her face.

Her name is Sadie, and she is eight years old. Sparkling periwinkle eyes view the world from a pretty heart-shaped face. Her long golden hair flows down her back in waves of loose curls.

Hopping out of bed, she runs down the hall, down the stairs, and into the kitchen, her face flushed with excitement because today is the first day of her summer vacation with her grandparents.

As Sadie races into the kitchen she says, "Good morning," and hops into her favorite chair.

For the last four years she has spent her summers with Baba, Papa, and Aunt Alece. Baba and Papa is what Sadie decided to call her grandparents when she first learned to talk. Her grandparents live in the mountains in a nice roomy cabin that was built by Baba's grandfather many years ago. The cabin itself was built on one end of a large meadow that is surrounded by a magnificent forest.

Sadie is by nature a very curious child with a lot of energy. Full of happiness and sometimes mischief, she often dreams about going on grand adventures to strange and wonderful places. Her favorite way to pass the time while visiting her grandparents is to go for long walks through the forest to the lake with Baba and Aunt Alece.

It's Monday morning, and not wanting to waste a minute of her vacation, she asks, "Can we all go for a walk to the lake when we finish eating?"

"Sorry, kiddo," her aunt Alece says. "It's finals week for me, and I have a lot of studying to do." With a slice of toast in one hand she picks up her backpack with the other and slings it over her shoulder. Stopping to give Sadie a quick kiss on the top of her head, she says, "I promise after finals I'm all yours for the rest of the summer." Lowering her voice, she whispers, "I'll be home by seven; until then no funny business, okay?"

"I'll try," Sadie whispers, feeling that sometimes it's hard to behave when life gets boring.

"Love you, Princess!" Her aunt Alece rushes out the door yelling, "Bye!"

Sadie looks at Baba and smiles. "Since Papa's already gone to work, I guess it's just you and me today."

Baba puts a plate of pancakes and bacon in front of Sadie and sits down next to her with a cup of coffee. "Oh, I'm sure we'll have lots of fun on our own today. Besides, I'm glad I get you all to myself on your first day here. You know how greedy I am when it comes to spending time alone with you."

Sadie digs into her pancakes and says between mouthfuls, "I had that dream again last night. The same one I have every year my first night here. Don't you think that's weird, Baba?"

"I don't know, Sadie. I think it just means that you're happy to be here. Don't think too much about it; dreams are often strange or weird."

"I know, but I only have it once a year, and it just seems so real, you know? It's kinda creepy, don't you think?"

"Not at all. I used to have strange dreams when I was your age. They don't mean anything. Besides, didn't you say that it's a happy dream? That you feel peaceful and happy in it?"

"Yes. I guess you're right. It's just that it stays with me for a while after I wake up, and the rest of my dreams don't do that."

After cleaning up the breakfast dishes, Sadie heads back upstairs to get dressed. Baba had unpacked her clothes the night before and hung them in the closet. As she's picking out her clothes she sees a box on the floor at the back of her closet. Dragging it out and opening it, she squeals in delight, "My toys!" Taking a moment to look through the box, she picks out her favorite dolls and then sits down on the floor. Digging further down through the box, she finds more outfits to dress them in. Laying them on the floor, she sits back to watch the show. She concentrates, picturing in her mind what she wants her dolls to do. "Dance," she says.

The dolls spring to life and start dancing around in a circle. Sadie claps her hands as the dolls spin and dance with one another. She bobs her head up and down and from side to side in rhythm to a song that's playing in her mind. With her finger she directs the dolls as they dance. She's played like this many times before, but only when she's alone or with her aunt Alece.

Her aunt Alece always says, "Don't tell anyone that you can do special things, Sadie. Because they won't understand, and it might even scare them." So Sadie is very careful to make sure that no one else is around when she plays in her special way.

Hearing Baba call her name, she says, "Time to get back in the box."

She has her dolls dance their way back to the box and one by one jump inside. She quickly finishes dressing and runs down the stairs.

It's late spring in the mountains, and the morning is warm with a light, cool breeze blowing. Sadie has always loved the mountains, and she can smell sunshine and wildflowers as she takes a deep breath. Feeling warm and happy, Sadie and Baba begin their walk.

"The air is much cooler in the forest," Sadie says.

"That's because the warm rays of the sun are blocked by all the trees branches."

The pungent smells of earth, pine, and wildflowers greet them as they venture deeper into the forest. Sadie looks up to see Baba smiling down at her, happiness and love shining in her eyes. She takes hold of Baba's hand as they walk in silence for a while listening to all the different bird calls.

"Do you remember what I told you about walking in the forest, Sadie?"

"Yes, Baba. If I wish to see any animals or possibly a fairy, I have to walk quietly. Because animals and fairies have excellent hearing, and talking or making loud noises will scare them off."

"That's right!"

Being eight years old, Sadie finds it hard to stay quiet for long periods of time. To help herself she likes to pretend that she's a fairy and the forest is sick and it's her job to make it better.

So while they're walking, being very careful that Baba doesn't see, Sadie changes the color of some of the flowers as she walks by. Touching each flower with her fingertip she whispers, "Pink, yellow, and you would defiantly look better if you were periwinkle!" she says as she passes a flower that's brown and wilted.

Finding an acorn on the ground, she tosses it at a tree. Pointing her finger, she rolls the acorn up its trunk and along a branch so she can watch a squirrel chase it.

They walk to the lake at least once a week while she's visiting, but today Sadie thinks the forest feels different somehow. She feels the hair on her arms stand on end.

"My skin has goose bumps," she mumbles.

"What did you say, sweetie?"

"I said I have goose bumps. All the hair on my arms is standing on end, see!"

"That's because this is a magical forest where the fairy folk live in a hidden world, a secret place where humans can't see them."

"You always say that, Baba."

"Have I told you that they sneak into our world once in a while to take care of the forest and the creatures that live here? That you need a special rock with a hole worn through the middle of it to see them?"

"No. How do they get here?"

"My grandmother told me that they ride into our world on moonbeams. So it's only when the moon is full and you have a rock with a hole in the middle of it to look through that you can see them. The hole in the rock must be made by Mother Nature and not man-made for it to work."

"Well, in that case, when we get to the lake I'm going to look for a rock with a hole in it," Sadie says.

It isn't long before boredom sets in. Sadie wonders why she can't tell Baba about all the special things she can do. If she wanted to she could pick a wildflower and make it dance and fly around just like a fairy.

She's sure Baba wouldn't be scared, but Aunt Alece says, "It just isn't the right time, Sadie. One day soon, I promise."

Picking a flower, she twirls it between her fingers. With a mischievous glint in her eyes she sneaks a quick peek at Baba to make sure she isn't watching. Dropping her arm to her side, she floats the flower back behind Baba. Slowing down just a bit, she allows Baba to get a step or two ahead of her. Suddenly the flower pops up suspended in midair just above Baba's head. Wiggling her finger, Sadie makes the flower fly in a circle around Baba's head like a bee buzzing around a flower. Baba swats at it as Sadie giggles.

"What are you giggling about?"

"You!" Sadie says as she has the flower make another pass around Baba's head. Baba swats at it again; then Sadie makes it touch her ear, and that really sets Baba off.

She swats at her ear as she ducks her head, squealing, "Oh! For heaven's sake!"

The flower dive bombs her head, zipping right past her nose, causing Baba to rear back as she swats at the air in front of her face. "I think this crazy bee has it out for me!"

While Baba looks all around for the bee, Sadie makes the flower zip past her head again, Baba waves both of her hands around her head trying to smack it away saying, "What the?"

The flower continues to attack from above. "Oh my!" Baba says as she ducks her head again, swatting at it.

Sadie just giggles as the flower makes another pass, circling Baba's head a couple of times.

"For crying out loud!" Baba says, running around, waving, and flapping her arms all around her body before darting up the path trying to get away from it, yelling, "You crazy bee!"

Bubbling laughter erupts from Sadie. As she loses her concentration the flower floats down to softly land on Baba's head.

Quickly Baba snatches it off and, opening her hand, says, "Well, for heaven's sake, it's just a flower! Would you look at that! Is this why you were laughing?" she says, holding up the flower.

Laughing and giggling, Sadie says, "You should have seen yourself, Baba! You were funny, running around with your arms flapping all around you." Sadie dances around in a circle, flapping her arms all around herself and mimicking Baba. "It was funny!"

"Why you little stinker. You knew it was a flower all along, didn't you? I wonder how it was flying around my head all that time. It must have been caught on a silk strand from a spider's web or something."

Still smiling, Sadie just shrugs. Feeling a small twinge of guilt, she quickly brushes the feeling away and says, "Something, I guess."

A short time later the path they are on ends abruptly at a large boulder. Stepping around it and out of the forest, they find themselves in a beautiful meadow. It's filled with soft green grass and mountain wildflowers in all colors, shapes, and sizes. At its center is a crystal blue lake. The lake itself isn't very deep, but the water is clear and cool. The first time Baba brought Sadie here she explained that this lake is fed by an underground spring, so the water is always fresh and clean.

Breaking into a run, Sadie heads straight for the lake itself. Stopping to stand at the edge, she leans over and looks down. She can see a small school of tiny fish staying close together right at the edge where the grass grows over the side and dangles down into the water. She knows that the tiny fish are hiding there so the bigger fish won't find them and gobble them up. Standing up, she puts her hand to her brow to block the sun.

"Look, Baba!" Sadie squeals. "Look at all the giant lily pads!"

"Wow! There are so many of them, and they're all just beautiful!" Baba says.

On the top of each lily pad are big vibrant flowers in bright yellows, pinks, reds, and white. Every once in a while they find a flower that is just the right blend of blue and purple to make it periwinkle. It's Sadie's favorite color, and she likes to pretend that periwinkle is a magical color created by fairies, which makes it even more special in her opinion.

Smiling, Sadie takes Baba's hand as they start their walk around the lake. They are on the lookout for nests of duck eggs, strange-looking insects, frogs, toads, and paw prints made by animals that come to the lake for a cool drink of water. She also likes to look for pretty rocks, and she keeps a baggie in her pocket to carry them home in. Walking side by side, they stop now and then to examine something of interest. It's Sadie's job to keep track of everything they find. Walking up to a bunch of flowers, Sadie reaches out to pick a few and then stops. Examining the flower, she notices that something about its stem doesn't look quite right. She bends down for a closer look as something moves all on its own. Sadie squeals and lets go.

Coming up behind her and chuckling, Baba says, "It's just a bug, Sadie. It's called a walking stick because it looks like a stick. They don't bite." Baba puts her hand down and coaxes the little bug onto the back of her hand. "See, it's not scary; as a matter of fact it kind of tickles when it walks. Do you want to hold it?"

Sadie takes a closer look at the bug. "No thanks, Baba. I'll wait till next time."

Putting the little bug back, Baba watches as Sadie runs off to find something else.

Every few minutes Sadie sounds off, calling out, "Baba, come look at this" or "Baba, what's that?"

On the other side of the lake just a few feet from the water's edge, Sadie is just starting to look for a rock with a hole in it when she finds a row of flat rocks lying in the grass. She starts jumping on them one after another, but as she jumps on the last one her feet sink right into it. Surprised and a little horrified, she starts screaming, "Baba! Baba, what's this I'm standing in?"

Walking up next to Sadie, Baba looks down and starts laughing. "That's a cow pie, Sadie."

Looking up at Baba and wrinkling her nose, she asks, "A cow pie? I thought it was a rock!"

"Come on. We'd better go wash your shoes off in the lake."

Pulling first one foot and then the other out of the cow pie, Sadie says, "Oh, Baba, this is so gross!" She huffs and stalks off into the water, mumbling, "I wish I could do something special about this right now!"

"Swish your feet back and forth in the water, Sadie; it will help to wash it off."

Looking down at her feet, she swishes them back and forth, complaining loudly, "This is absolutely disgusting—my shoes are ruined! Now we have to go home, Baba! I can't wear shoes that have been in *cow poop*! It's not coming off!" she whines.

"All in all, I think it's been a fun morning, don't you?" Baba asks.

"I guess," Sadie grumps.

"You found three duck nests, a lady bug, two furry caterpillars, that walking stick, and a pretty pink rock," Baba says, trying to distract her.

"Yes, but now my shoes have *poop* on them, Baba. And I have to walk all the way home in *poopy* shoes. That's not very fun! And I didn't even get to find a rock with a hole in it yet!" she says as she walks out of the water.

Smiling to herself, Baba asks, "What would you like for lunch?"

But before Sadie can answer, she hears a gravelly voice croak, "Help me! Help me, please!"

Stopping, she looks up at Baba and asks, "Did you hear that?"

"Hear what?" Baba says.

Standing still, they listen for another minute, and sure enough there it is again—a very weak "Help me. Help me, please! Can you hear me?"

This time Baba hears it too. The voice continues to call to them, "I'm over here. Help me, please!"

Following the sound of that strange gravelly croaking, they find it coming from a colony of lily pads floating not too far from them at the water's edge.

## MR. FROG

Walking over to the edge of the water, they look around and see lying on a giant lily pad a very large, very green frog. Lying on his back, he looks up at them and blinks his big yellow eyes and then says, "I'm so glad you heard me! I had given up hope that anyone would!"

They both just stand there looking down at the big green frog, unable to believe what they are hearing and seeing. They have been to the lake many times, and never before have they met a talking frog.

The frog, not noticing their surprise, continues talking. "I have been lying on this lily pad for such a long time. You see, I hurt my leg while catching bugs for my breakfast. I'm so glad you heard me. Do you think you can help me?"

Sadie, realizing that they are just standing there and staring at him, says, "I'm sure we can, but how are you talking to us?"

Looking up at them, the frog asks, "What do you mean? How am I talking to you? I talk to fairies all the time."

"What fairies?" Sadie asks.

The frog, looking very puzzled, replies, "The fairies that take care of the forest, of course. Don't you live here with them?"

Sadie looks up at Baba with wide questioning eyes. Baba looks from Sadie to the frog and says, "No. We live in a house in the meadow at the edge of the forest."

Sadie, having forgotten all about her shoes, remembers that the frog asked them for help. Thinking that he might be in pain from his hurt leg, she asks, "What can we do to help you, uh, sir?"

"Yes, yes that's right!" he replies. "Please, call me Mr. Frog. If you can take the time to carry me back to my home—it's just over there—I would be very grateful!" He points to a large formation of rocks stacked at the water's edge across the lake. "I don't feel safe out in the open like this!" He nervously looks around. "I'm very lucky that nothing has come along and gobbled me up."

Understanding his situation, Baba very gently picks him up. She is surprised to find that he is much heavier than she expected him to be. She carefully carries Mr. Frog around the lake and gently lays him down on a giant lily pad that's floating in front of the opening to his home and peaks inside. She can see that the interior is quite large.

"This looks very cozy and comfortable," Baba remarks.

"Oh, it is. It's very comfortable." Mr. Frog, being grateful for their help, wants to offer them something in return. Feeling very distressed over the problem of not having anything to give them, he says, "I have nothing to give you at this time. Is there something that I can do for you instead?"

Sadie and Baba look at each other and smile. Looking down at Mr. Frog, Baba says, "A simple thank you is enough, Mr. Frog."

"Our customs are very different here in the forest," he explains. "We believe that the words 'thank you' are a verbal expression that is empty and meaningless. Fairies feel that gifts given to remember kind deeds are much more meaningful."

They look at each other, knowing exactly what he can do for them. "In return for our help we would like to meet a fairy," Sadie says.

Mr. Frog, not seeing any harm in their request, says, "If you return in two days at sunrise I will take you to meet the fairies." Mr. Frog is sure that his leg will be much better by the morning, and he needs at least a day to travel deep into the forest to get a "silver bough."

A silver bough is a branch cut from a rare and very special silver pine. It's used to create a portal, an opening between the fairy and human worlds that allows both humans and fairies to pass back and forth. Mr. Frog is sure that Princess Serena will be able to sense the magic in the little girl just as he can.

Saying their good-byes, Sadie and Baba hurry home, hungry and excited.

The next morning Mr. Frog wakes early and stretches his leg to test it. He finds that it is much better than he hoped it would be. Having missed his dinner the night before, he is very hungry and in a hurry to be out catching his breakfast. He leaps out of his home, and his splash into the lake creates rings of ripples that grow larger as they expand outward, rolling toward the opposite shore. Swimming out into open water, he finds the lake smooth as glass, and it feels good to be skimming across its surface. There are always fat juicy bugs on the lily pads in the early morning, so he swims toward the nearest group. It doesn't take him long to fill his tummy.

Satisfied, Mr. Frog feels that he's ready to start his journey. He doesn't normally travel very far from his home, but he knows that humans can only pass through to the hidden world with a silver bough in their possession. He's never taken a human to see the fairies before. "The little girl, by herself, would be able to pass through just fine without it," he says out loud.

Only the queen of the fairy folk has ever given the silver bough to a human that he knows of. "It's only on very rare occasions and only to a human that she deems worthy," he says, rubbing his chin thoughtfully. Mr. Frog, having lived alone for so long often, speaks out loud when thinking.

Remembering the queen, he wonders if he's made a mistake in telling Sadie and Baba that he can take them to meet the fairies. He thinks for just a minute and then decides that he really has no choice. Besides, he is looking forward to seeing Princess Serena and her family again. "Come to think of it, the little girl Sadie bears a striking resemblance to Princess Serena's daughter, Lila." Shaking off his doubts, Mr. Frog, knowing that he has a long way to go and only a short time to complete his journey, hurries his pace by hopping great lengths to increase his speed.

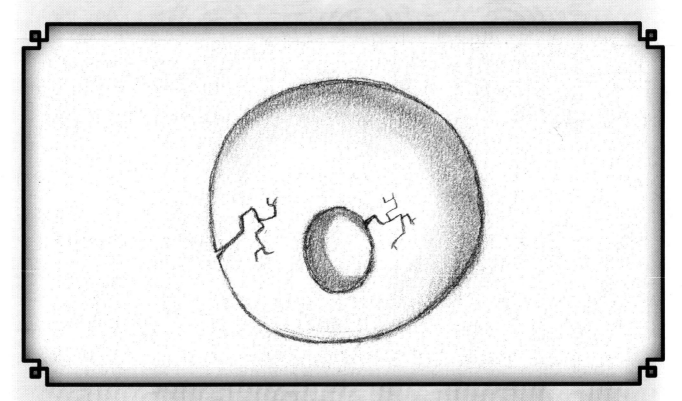

# FOLKLORE (THE FAE)

At home Sadie is so excited about all that has happened and the adventure they will be going on that she talks nonstop throughout the day and finds it hard to fall asleep that night.

Lying in her bed, wide awake, she can't stop thinking about fairies. "I am actually going to get to meet some fairies," she says, talking out loud to herself. "I'm so excited, my stomach feels all squirmy inside! I'm not gonna be able to fall asleep tonight! I wonder what they will look like. Tiny little fairies with wings?"

Finally, around midnight, Baba, having listened to Sadie talking to herself all night, fixes her a warm cup of milk, knowing that it will calm her down and help her get to sleep.

The next morning after breakfast Sadie asks Baba what she should put in their backpack, not knowing what they might need for their trip. Baba suggests that they do some research on the computer to see what, if anything, they can find out about fairy folk. Sadie thinks this is an excellent idea. They decide the best place to start is by typing in "fairy folk," and the computer screen fills with a wealth of information. They find that most of the history on fairies comes from Irish folklore. Baba begins to read to Sadie all the lore she can find on the website.

"It says that elves, gnomes, sprites, pixies, bogarts, brownies, leprechauns, goblins, and many other creatures are all just different types of fairy or fae. Sprites, pixies and others like them have wings. The rest don't need them. They all use magic, and their powers vary. This says that there are royal fairies known as the Sidhe. Also referred to as the first race, all other fairies or fae come from them. Royals or Sidhe are normal in height just like us, and they are ancient and very, very powerful! Nothing from our world can kill them, but iron burns them and makes them weak."

"Ancient? What does that mean?" Sadie asks.

"It means that they are much older than the human race. It says that they have pointy ears, they're all very beautiful, and their skin gives off a golden glow. They have golden hair, and their eyes are always some shade of blue. They live in troops. That must be what they call a family or maybe a small village?"

"Golden hair and blue eyes," Sadie says. "Hmm, I have golden hair, and my eyes are kinda blue!"

Lost in their research, they don't notice how dark it has become outside until they hear Papa, home from work, come through the front door.

"Hello!" he calls. "Anyone home!" Turning on a light, he wonders why it's so dark in the house and why he doesn't smell dinner cooking like he usually does.

Sadie hops down from her chair and runs to him, yelling, "Papa, Papa you're home!"

Jumping into his outstretched arms, she gives him a big hug. He is always amazed at the swell of love and pride he feels every time he holds her. "You feel so small in my arms," he tells her.

"That's because I might be a fairy," Sadie says. "That and you're so big, Papa."

Papa, standing six and a half feet tall, is much bigger than most men. "Is that so? And here I thought you were just a munchkin," he says.

Sadie giggles, saying, "I'm not a munchkin, Papa. They never get any bigger than what I am right now. But fairies grow to be as big as normal people."

"And just how do you know so much about fairies all of a sudden?" Papa asks.

"Baba and I have been reading about them on the computer."

"You have?" Papa says as he tickles her. Sadie squeals and laughs as Baba walks into the room.

As he puts Sadie down to give his wife a hug, his tummy growls and he asks, "Why isn't dinner cooking?"

"I thought it would be fun to go out for a pizza."

Papa, being hungry after a long day at work and not having had pizza in a while, says, "That sounds like a good idea. Just give me a few minutes to get washed up and change my clothes."

On the way into town Sadie can't stop talking about fairies. On and on she talks, making Baba and Papa laugh.

After they order their pizza Sadie says, "Oh, Papa, I forgot to tell you—we met a really big talking frog today."

"You did?" he replies, smiling. Papa thinks that this is just another one of her stories she's so fond of telling.

"Yes, a big one, huh Baba?"

"We sure did! A big green one with bright yellow eyes!"

Papa realizes that she isn't joking. "You're telling me that the two of you actually met a giant talking frog today?"

"Well, I wouldn't say he was a giant; just really big for a frog," Baba says.

"He was a real pretty green color too!" Sadie states as a matter of fact. "His name is Mr. Frog."

Baba, wanting to change the subject, tells Sadie, "Why don't we leave some of the story for later? You'd better eat up so we can get home; your aunt Alece will be there soon."

"Yay, Aunt Alece. I can't wait to tell her that I might be a real fairy and we met a talking frog."

As Sadie eats her pizza, Baba gives Papa the look that says, "We'll talk later."

That night sleep comes easier for Sadie, as she has a tummy full of pizza and is tired after all the research that she helped Baba with. Sadie wants to tell Aunt Alece, but she hasn't come home from school by the time Sadie is ready for bed.

After tucking Sadie into bed, Baba and Papa go down into the kitchen. "Okay what's going on?" Papa asks. "What's this business about a talking green frog?"

"I couldn't believe it either, and I was there talking to him. I carried him around the lake, and let me tell you, he was much heavier than he looked," Baba says, a bit exasperated.

Papa, smiling because of the look on his wife's face, says, "Really? What's this about Sadie thinking she's a fairy?"

"Oh, that. Well, the lore says that royal fairies have golden hair and varying shades of blue eyes like her. It's okay—she's only eight. Besides, that big green frog talking to us didn't help matters! He says he can take us the meet the fairies. Real ones!"

Papa, a surprised look on his face, says, "You don't actually believe you can go there, do you? I mean—Oh, I don't know what I mean! This can't be real!"

"According to Mr. Frog it is!"

They look at each other, neither knowing what to say. Thinking, Baba says, "I'd better see what Sadie put in the backpack."

Baba finds the backpack on the floor by the computer. Opening it, she looks through it and starts listing everything she finds out loud. "Camera, extra shoes, and socks." Baba smiles, remembering yesterday. Continuing, she says, "Sadie's fairy wings, her fairy wand, a bag full of play jewelry with a note marked 'gifts' in Sadie's handwriting, a bag of peanut M&M's, a bag of Skittles, a bottle of water, and her stuffed monkey." Baba can't help herself; she starts laughing.

In the morning after a quick breakfast they dress quietly because Papa and Aunt Alece are still sleeping. Since Sadie packed their backpack the night before they manage to slip out of the house without waking the others. Baba leaves a note for Papa telling him not to worry.

With Sadie in charge of the flashlight and Baba carrying their backpack, they make their way through the forest as quickly as they can. The sun is just coming up, painting the sky a wonderful reddish-orange color as they step into the meadow.

Seeing Mr. Frog waiting for them by the lake, they start walking toward him. On the ground, in front of his feet, Sadie spies something that looks like a tree branch.

"Good morning!" he calls. "Right on time, I see."

Sadie is so excited she can hardly breathe. "Good morning!" she calls back as she waves her arm excitedly.

Mr. Frog, not wanting to waste any time, starts explaining what the silver bough is and what it is used for. He tells them a brief story about Princess Serena, filling in the facts as he recalls them:

"When Princess Serena was a young girl she would sneak into the human world to observe them. She found your customs of family units quite interesting. She would dream of the day when she could be mated and start a family of her own. So after she was mated to Rowan she told him about her dreams, Rowan, wanting to make her happy, agreed to leave with her and start their own family and fairy troop. They searched throughout the different realms until they found the perfect forest. Once they decided to remain here the princess planted her own silver pine somewhere in this forest. Princess Serena once told me that for some unknown reason this forest seemed to call to her in a subtle but undeniable way. I'm not real sure what she meant by that! Anyway, unlike the other members of their race, Princess Serena and her family enjoy the company of others."

"Royal fairies don't like the other fairies?" Sadie asks.

"It's not that they don't like them; they just prefer to live amongst their own kind or by themselves. She's a very nice fairy; you'll like her. You look a lot like her daughter, Lila, as a matter of fact!"

Done with his story, he asks Baba, "Could you put the silver bough in your bag?"

This is not an easy task, because the branch is about two feet long and bushy. With everything Sadie has packed they don't have much room left in their pack, and Baba has to rearrange everything to make it fit. Completing her task, she looks over at Sadie and says, holding out her hand, "Ready?"

As they leave the meadow and the lake behind Mr. Frog tells them that there are no paths to follow and they should try to keep up. "There are only a few places we can open a portal, and the nearest one isn't too far away." True to his word it doesn't take long to reach a part of the river where huge boulders force the water to flow around them, creating a wide sandy beach on the other side.

Mr. Frog immediately gets to work gathering rocks, branches, and small bunches of wildflowers. He arranges them in a semicircle at the river's edge and then asks Baba, "Could you bring me the silver bough from your bag? Now we must all stand together in the semicircle and hold hands." He places the silver bough at their feet and begins to chant in a sing-song voice, which sounds really funny as he croaks:

*"As the water flows from the falls,*
*Let the silver bough break down the walls.*

> *Three to pass through this gate.*
> *A traveler's woes may be their fate.*
> *Enter all with happy hearts,*
> *For this is where adventure starts."*

Suddenly the branch starts to shimmer in a silvery color all on its own, and to their surprise the air in front of them becomes wavy and distorted. They're unable to see the opposite side of the river because an opening has formed in the air just above the water's edge. Inside the opening is a swirling mass of white fog. Moving closer, Sadie tries to get a better look inside.

"It looks so strange, like a moving picture someone put in the air. There's no back to it, Baba. I can see behind it! But I can't see anything inside except the fog."

Mr. Frog hops up to the portal and turns to Sadie and Baba. He notices a mild look of apprehension on Baba's face and reassures her, "Don't worry. It's perfectly safe; no harm will come to you," he tells her. He then turns around and hops straight up into the air, and immediately he is sucked into the portal and is gone.

Baba and Sadie, standing very still, gaze into the portal. Baba looks down at Sadie and says, "It's now or never, sweetheart. I say we go for it!"

Hanging on tightly to each other's hand they jump straight up. Sadie and Baba feel the pull of the portal, and then they're falling. They try desperately to hang on to each other's hands as they tumble through fog, their bodies being pulled in different directions. The force pulling at them increases, and their hands slip free of one another's. Somewhere in the distance Sadie can hear Baba calling. She sounds a bit frantic, calling for her over and over again.

Sadie calls back to her, "I'm here, Baba, and I'm okay." Her body feels very strange, being stretched one second and then squished the next like modeling clay. Suddenly there's a bright flash of colorful lights, and just as it started her fall ends. She lands on her hands and knees in a soft fluffy substance that immediately becomes more solid. Taking a deep breath she looks around and sees that the fog is gone. She finds Baba just a few feet away on her hands and knees looking back at her.

Feeling safe on the ground, Sadie says, "Wow, that was a little scary but fun."

"Fun? You call that fun!" Baba says. "I just hope getting back is easier than that."

Standing, they hear a soft tinkling sound like wind chimes, and looking down they see golden seashells under their feet. Sadie can see that they're standing on a wide path or road paved in the golden shells. "That's funny. I didn't notice these before when I was on my hands and knees!" she says, looking at Baba.

"I didn't notice them either." Looking up, Baba says, "The sun overhead is much brighter here, but it doesn't hurt the eyes and make you squint like it does at home."

Sadie looks around for her backpack and is unable to find it. "I don't see my backpack, Baba."

Baba looks around. "I don't see it either. Maybe it got lost in the fog. It might turn up later."

A beautiful butterfly zips by. It darts here and there, leaving a sparkling trail of mist like a streamer in its wake, and Sadie forgets about her backpack.

"Baba, have you ever seen a butterfly fly so fast? At home they always seem to kind of float by." Looking around she sees quite a number of them flying back and forth between the forest and the town.

Out of nowhere Mr. Frog hops up to them and, smiling, says, "Welcome to the realm of Fairywinkle, nestled in the heart of Nocturnal Forest, at the base of Mystic Mountain, home to Princess Serena and her family. Are you ready to meet some fairies?"

# FAIRY FOLK (THE FAE)

All around her Sadie can see that everything is slightly different than at home. Strange-looking birds in the most unusual iridescent colors fly back and forth between the town and forest, these too leaving trails of sparkling mist behind them.

"Wow, did you see that? Everything sure does fly a lot faster here, and would you look at all the flowers. Their colors are so much prettier here than at home!" Sadie says in awe.

"Do you smell that?"

"Smell what?" Sadie asks, quickly covering her nose.

"The air! It smells so clean!" Baba says with wonder in her voice.

"Oh, Baba. I thought you meant something stinky."

The path they're on starts at the tree line and leads to a small village in the middle of a clearing encircled by forest. As Sadie looks more closely she can see that the shells spread out from the road to form a ring around the village with several paths leading into the forest. Looking down at her feet, she sweeps the toe of her shoe back and forth in the golden shells. This action produces the same sound she heard when she got to her feet: wind chimes. "What's with all the shells?" Sadie asks Mr. Frog.

"The shells are from Princess Serena's favorite beach! She loves the sound they make," he replies. "They also serve as a warning system for the town—the forest isn't safe at night."

Another butterfly zips past the end of Sadie's nose, this time encircling her head, wrapping the stream of sparkling color around her and then flying straight up into the air and out of sight.

"Look, Baba," Sadie says, touching the sparkling mist. "It's sticking to my finger!" She waves her hand through the air, making her own design. Smiling, she feels happy and peaceful. "For the first time in my life I feel like I belong, like this is where I'm supposed to be, Baba." Twirling around in a circle, her arms stretched high above her head, she starts to laugh.

Baba doesn't quite know what she means by that. Brushing the comment aside for now, she is eager to start exploring this world with Sadie. When she was growing up, her own grandmother often told her stories about fairies and their hidden world, which is why she enjoys sharing those stories with Sadie.

The light musical sound from the shells follows them as they walk to the village. Golden dust rises behind their footsteps as they walk. Unnoticed, the strange butterflies and birds swoop down to bathe their wings in it. As they get closer Sadie can see that there are only five houses in the small village. Each house has its own unique design. The small houses are set back from the road with large yards that are beautifully designed and neatly groomed. At the end of the road is the largest and the most beautiful house of all. Walking toward it, Sadie notices that it seems to shimmer and change its shape ever so slightly. It continues to do this every couple of minutes as they approach.

Mr. Frog says, "This is the home of Princess Serena, her mate, Rowan, and their daughter, Lila."

Coming to the edge of the yard, they can see that the bushes are all trimmed to look like whimsical creatures. Sadie, pointing, says, "Look at that, Mr. Frog. That bush looks just like you!" As she says this she notices three little men working on one of the bushes across the yard, and she waves at them. "Who are they?" she asks Mr. Frog.

"Those are the elf brothers. They tend the gardens here. I don't remember their names—it's been a long time—but they do beautiful work, don't they?"

"They certainly do!" Baba says, looking over Sadie's shoulder.

As they're looking and pointing at all the different shapes of bushes in the yard, the air a few feet in front of them begins to sparkle and then distorts and begins to roll like waves as three beautiful people walk through it.

"It's like some kind of weird door, and the people are all golden and shiny," Sadie whispers.

A woman, her face so beautiful it almost hurts to look upon it, glides down the walkway. Her skin is a honey-gold color, and tall and slender she walks with her head held high, moving with the confidence and grace that you would expect of royalty. Her eyes are the exact same shade of periwinkle as Sadie's, and her long golden hair shines with a light of its own.

The man beside her is tall and powerfully built, handsome beyond reason with golden brown skin. His long wavy blonde hair shines in the sunlight. Sadie is unable to look away from him for a moment as the power of his gaze holds her attention. Piercing blue eyes the color of glacial ice stare back at her, his stare making her mind tingle with familiarity.

Finally able to look away, it's the young girl walking toward her whom Sadie gapes at. Blinking her eyes once, then twice, she whispers, "It's like looking in a mirror; she looks exactly like me."

Lila stops just inches away from Sadie and then reaches out to touch her, unable to believe that she is real and standing right in front of her. Looking over at her mother, she asks, "How can what I am seeing be possible? I don't understand!"

Sadie stands very still, afraid to breathe. "This is not a dream. This is not a dream," she whispers. Chancing a sideways glance at Baba, she sees that Baba is just staring wide-eyed at all of them.

Princess Serena turns to her mate, Rowan, and asks, "Do you have an explanation for what we are seeing?" But she can tell that he is just as stunned as she is.

Mentally shaking himself, Rowan is the first to recover, saying, "I think it would be best if we all go inside."

One minute Sadie is standing in the yard and the next minute she is inside the strange beautiful house standing in a room with a very high ceiling and a large open area. She starts walking through the room looking at all of the odd, beautiful things. Candles as tall as light posts are carved into exotic beasts, their flames flickering in strange beautiful colors. Giant vases full of lovely flowers the size of Sadie's head and bigger are placed strategically throughout the room, giving off a wonderful scent that's very soothing. Beautifully carved wood furniture with big soft-looking pillows in the prettiest pastel colors are arranged facing each other in a cozy seating area.

Taking a seat on one of the couches, she sinks into the soft marshmallow-like pillows. She can't ignore the electrifying sensation that's been flowing across her skin and coursing through her mind since she first looked into the man's eyes. It's like having goose bumps inside and out. The feeling is even stronger now that she isn't occupied with exploring the room. Rubbing her hands up and down her arms, she says, "This feels really weird!"

Baba, still standing in the same place where she first appeared in the house, her eyes popping, says, "Magnificent, truly magnificent!"

Sitting on the couch, Sadie sees a flash of sparkling color zip past. "It's one of those big butterflies, and it's flying straight to the beautiful lady!" Sadie yells as she points and waves her finger in Princess Serena's direction.

Stopping a few inches from the princess's face, it whispers something to her as it hovers in midair.

"Baba look—the beautiful lady is talking to that butterfly!"

That's when Sadie realizes that it's not a butterfly. "Oh, my, gosh, Baba! It's not a butterfly at all, but a little fairy," Sadie says, sitting straight up and scooting to the edge of the couch. "I knew it! I knew that fairies would be small and have wings!" she blurts out loud.

Baba, stifling a laugh, just smiles. The small fairy is only a few inches tall. She has thin wispy antennae protruding from her forehead, large dark iridescent eyes, and gossamer wings that appear to be made of gold and silver dust. The wings are just a little longer than she is tall.

"Her wings are what makes the sparkling mist!" Sadie says. Watching the little fairy, she can see just a small amount of the dust falling off her wings as she hangs in midair.

Finishing their conversation, the little fairy zips off, flying just above Sadie's head and into another room, leaving a trail behind her. Sadie reaches up and pokes her finger into the trail. Smiling, she draws circles and hearts in the air until it disappears.

Sadie doesn't quite know what to think of all that's happening. Looking at Rowan, she says, "It's very strange to meet someone who looks exactly like yourself, and all of you have been staring at me since we were outside. I've always been told that it's rude to stare at someone, especially a guest in your home." Still feeling very uncomfortable, she wishes they would all stop staring at her. As soon as she thinks it, their eyes shift away from her; they seem startled by this for some reason. But Sadie's just glad that they stopped staring at her.

Lila, sitting quietly and watching everything that's been transpiring, just giggles.

Serena and Rowan look at each other, their eyes communicating what they dare not say out loud, *Our child has power, great power.*

Princess Serena, unable to stand the suspense of not knowing what this is all about, announces, "I am going to Avendale! That is where my mother, Queen Aurelia, lives. I need to speak with her about what has happened!" Princess Serena is convinced that this can't be just a coincidence. Her mother knows what this is all about; she is sure of that if nothing else.

Looking into her daughter's eyes, she knows that there can be no other explanation other than that Sadie is Lila's twin. Walking over to Lila, she kneels down in front of her and gently takes her hand, saying, "You see, my sweet, when you were born you had a twin sister. My mother told us that one of our daughters had died. This is not uncommon, because even though we become immortal, there is a brief time after we are born when we are fragile. Not bound to any magic. It is during this time that many of our kind perish. Twins are extremely rare, and it is almost unheard of for even one of the children to survive. So even though we were grieving for the loss of one daughter, we felt blessed that we still had you. Lila dear, we never told you about the twin you would never know because we didn't want you to suffer her loss as we had."

"But I have always felt a loss, Mother! My heart has always ached for something that was missing in my life; I just didn't know what." Lila looks down at her hands in her lap for a moment. Looking back up at her mother she says, "There have been many times in my life when I have felt lonely and wished I had a sister to play with and tell my secrets to. A sister I could share adventures with or talk too late at night when I cannot sleep."

Princess Serena had to remind herself that although adult fairies don't need to sleep, child fairies do. It's while they are sleeping that their magic recharges and grows more powerful. It becomes a part of them, fusing with their mind so they can use it with just a thought whenever they need to. As they grow older they learn the more powerful spells from their parents, and sometimes other much older fairies teach them a spell or two as well.

# THE BLENDING

Looking over at Sadie sitting on the couch listening to what's being said, looking all alone and decidedly uncomfortable, a very strong feeling or a longing to be near her blossoms inside Lila. Letting go of her mother's hand, she walks over to the couch and sits down next to Sadie. Smiling, they study each other for a long moment, looking into one another's eyes, eyes the same shade as their mother's, searching each other's faces, looking for any small difference.

As if finding out you had an identical twin isn't enough, they are suddenly able to hear one another's thoughts. At first they don't know what to do. Their thoughts are somewhat jumbled and confusing, like two people talking really fast at the same time. Unexpectedly having another person join you inside your mind is very unsettling, the experience foreign and strange. It's as if their minds are blending together becoming one but still separate, because not only can each they hear the other's thoughts, but they are starting to share each other's memories as well. Startled, all they can do is sit and stare at each other wide-eyed, their bodies tense as their minds go through the process of the blending, coming to know each other's experiences as if they had been there living it themselves.

"This is a really strange feeling." Sadie giggles inside her head.

"I agree, but it's a wonderful feeling too, because for the first time in my life I feel complete! I have finally found my missing piece! You Sadie, you are my missing piece." Lila smiles as she looks into her sister's eyes.

After a few minutes the jumbled words and images sort themselves out and start flowing in a pattern that is comfortable for both girls.

Knowledge flows into Sadie, and she finally understands why she can do so many special things. She also knows now that she has the power to do so much more than she ever thought possible. All the information streaming back and forth between them seems to comfort her as acceptance settles in her mind. It doesn't take long before it all feels perfectly normal to both girls.

As the girls sit together, quietly communicating, Rowan and Serena get a chance to say good-bye. In a twinkling of lights Serena disappears.

Rowan, keeping an eye on the girls, says, "Come and have a seat with me, will you?"

"Thank you. I would love to."

"I want to try to answer some of the many questions you have," Rowan says, having already accepted the fact that Sadie is Lila's twin.

Baba sits quietly observing the exchange between the girls, and as she is watching they just suddenly vanish.

Panicked, Baba turns to Rowan, her eyes wide with alarm. He reaches out and gently pats her hand, saying, "They have just gone to Lila's room to play. All is well, I assure you." As he does this the little fairy returns to offer them some refreshments.

Baba, curious about what they eat and drink, accepts the offer. Without the little fairy returning, she suddenly feels something warm by her hand, and looking down she sees that the table is set with large mugs containing a wonderful-smelling liquid and a couple of plates full of what looks like different kinds of pastries spread out between them.

Taking hold of the mug, she raises it to her nose and sniffs the contents. Taking a sip, she smiles and says, "This is very good."

Rowan smiles. "I believe your people call it tea."

Rowan had been watching the girls as well, trying to push aside his own feelings of confusion, astonishment, and anger over this new reality. He has found it hard to take his own eyes off of them, all the longing he's felt for his dead daughter, all the love he's carried deep inside all these years rising to the surface. What he really wants to do is scoop the both of them into his arms, breathe in their scent, and hold them there until the ache in his chest recedes.

He looks into Baba's eyes, human eyes that have watched his daughter grow these past few years. She has loved and cared for his child, raising her as her own, not knowing all this time that Sadie was not of her world.

He listens as Baba rattles off first one question and then another. Chuckling at the woman's inquisitive nature, Rowan decides that it's best to start at the beginning even though she has already heard some of their tale.

Holding up his hand to stop the flow of questions, he says, "Sadie is Lila's twin, as you undoubtedly heard. Serena and I were told that she died shortly after her birth. We had no reason to doubt the queen."

"How awful it must have been for you. What's happening between the girls now?"

"Do not concern yourself—it is all perfectly normal. Fairy twins always share this blending of the minds. It is part of their physiology. Of course it usually happens gradually over time as they grow, with the blending being fully forged and complete within the first year of life."

"The fact that they've been apart all these years is making it happen all at once for them?"

"Yes. We all have the ability to read the minds of humans and the other races of the fae, but we cannot read each other's minds, except in the case of twins. We can sense one another and we can call to one another with our minds, but only as a feeling."

"Fascinating!" Baba says as she sips her tea.

"Twins can sense what the other is feeling no matter how far apart they are, but they can only read each other's thoughts when in close proximity to one another. Some fae have the ability to communicate across vast distances, but this is a rare power indeed, and only those that are Sidhe can achieve this."

"I know that the word 'fae' is used when talking about all the many different species of fairy folk, correct?"

"That is correct. Each species of fae has its own magic, the strength of which varies depending on the type of fairy. You see, our world's system is much like your Renaissance period but more advanced."

Rowan continues to answer her numerous questions as best he can about his people and the rest of the fae. There are just some things he either doesn't feel she will understand or she is not allowed to know.

When Princess Serena finally returns she notices that the girls are no longer in the room. Reaching out with her mind, she calls to them. They appear, sitting together on the couch, a mischievous glint in both their eyes. Wondering what they had been up to, she walks over to where the girls sit and gathers them in her arms, holding them as close as possible, breathing in their special scent, knowing in that moment what it feels like to finally be complete and at peace within herself. The pain and longing that she has kept deep inside flow out of her, being replaced by joy and happiness. The love for her lost daughter surfaces, filling her to near bursting.

Princess Serena quietly says, "I have spoken with your grandmother, the queen. She says that she separated the two of you at birth for your own protection. That both of you surviving was such a rare and wonderful event that the other powerful fairies coveted you and would have possibly tried to take one of you or kill you both. Either of those actions would have started a war, and that was something she could not allow. So she took one of you, Sadie, to the human world, hiding you there to keep you both safe. She then told everyone, including myself and your father, that our baby girl had died. That way all the other fairies would leave us alone, showing sympathy for us during our time of sorrow and grief."

Looking into both their eyes, she can tell that the girls are silently talking between themselves. Continuing, she tells them, "At that time, your grandmother did not feel there was any other way to protect both of you, and even though it tore at her heart and she grieved deeply over what she had to do, she knew that her baby granddaughters would be safe."

Looking at Sadie to make sure she understood her meaning, she continues, "She left you in the care of a human family whom she knew were kind and loving people. She then wove a powerful magic spell that would make them believe that you were theirs. At the same time she wove a cloak of protection around you that no other magic could penetrate, keeping you well hidden and ensuring your safety. Having done everything she could to keep you both safe, your grandmother felt she could live with what she had done."

Both girls listen closely to the story of their birth. They find it to be a very good story, full of adventure and intrigue.

Princess Serena is both surprised and pleased at how well the girls are taking all of this. "Over the years she kept a close eye on you, Sadie, and once a year under a spell of invisibility she would go and visit you."

"She did? When, when did she visit me? I'm pretty sure I would have remembered seeing a fairy queen!"

Princess Serena, smiling at her daughter, says, "In your dreams, my sweet! She visited you in your dreams!"

Wide-eyed, Sadie sits stunned for a moment, thinking. "I remember my dream that I always have the first night I come to visit Baba and Papa. A beautiful lady takes me to a beach and we talk and swim and eat wonderful food! Baba, my dream! My dream! It is real! Remember my dream? The one I have every year!"

"Yes, I remember. You just had it again a couple of days ago."

Finishing her talk with the girls, Princess Serena excuses herself and walks to where Rowan and the human woman sit, patiently waiting for her.

# THE DIFFERENCE BETWEEN LIGHT AND DARK

Sitting down, she begins her tale again, only this time telling all that she has learned. "I have explained to the children what they need to know."

"Sadie sure has accepted all of this really well," Baba says.

"It is much easier for children to accept—they are not yet set in their ways. Now, I must tell you that it was Kieran, king of the dark fairies, who had demanded one of our twin girls be brought to him so that he could raise her as his own heir."

"Kieran? He is why we lost our daughter? He is the cause of all of our pain?" Rowan thunders, his eyes flashing, and says in a low venomous voice. "I will crush him under the heel of my boot for this!"

She takes her mate's hand and squeezes it gently. "First let me explain to Sadie's Baba some of our ancient history. May I call you Baba?"

"I would like that very much! To both that is, the history and to you calling me Baba. I do have a question though. I've noticed that you don't refer to Kieran as King Kieran. Why is that?"

"He is not our king!" Rowan says heatedly. "He is only a king in his kingdom. The kingdom he made!" Rowan tells her with a slight sneer in his voice. "Not one earned or passed on by birth! He is quite simply a child with more power than he deserves! We do not recognize him as royal. He lost that when our queen banished him!"

"Yes, well," Princess Serena, says, looking first to Baba and then pointedly at her mate. Rowan just smiles politely in return. "Our race is called the Sidhe. Ours is a race much older than you humans. We have been around for many, many millennia. In the beginning our queens and kings lived in harmony for untold millennia, passing their titles down through their blood lines. We existed in great numbers at one time until the war between our people. You humans view us as immortal because nothing of your world has the ability to take our life. But in our world we can be killed by others of our kind. However, it is strictly forbidden unless you are protecting yourself or that of a loved one.

"As I was saying, the war lasted until my mother came into power, but by then many of our people were already gone. From the time my mother became queen there was peace among our people until Kieran became jealous of the fact that my mother and our line would always be more powerful than he was. He knew that she had the ability to infuse him with more power and make them equals. But each time he brought it up she refused him immediately, not even willing to discuss it. This did not sit well with him, as you might guess."

"Child, I tell you! Our queen should have stripped him of all his powers! Made him mortal—that would suit him, the pompous prig! A child or someone who acts like one should not possess great power!" Rowan roared.

"Yes, all would agree with you, my love." Princess Serena pats his hand.

"As millennia passed Kieran became more and more insistent, until finally my mother became bored with his constant whining about his lack of power. He knew as well as she did our race's history, how the males were the cause of the war between our people, and why it had been decided all those millennia ago that it would be the females of our race who would rule, entrusting the queen alone with the Tablet of Spells, our race's most powerful token. At that time all females were infused with greater power than the males, passing the royal blood line along from one female to another always. Kieran became so insistent that my mother didn't trust him anymore. She was forced to hide the Tablet of Spells to protect it from Kieran or one of his spies."

"This is all so fascinating! What is the Tablet of Spells?

"It is a golden rune stone that possesses all of our spells. Put quite simply, it is what gives us our power, our magic as you would say."

"In our world we have a lot of lore about fairies. I don't know if it's all correct, but we humans have believed in fairies for centuries."

"I remember that when I was young, I would sneak into the human world as one of you. My mother would become so angry with me when she found out, but I didn't care!" The princess smiles as she says this. "I have always loved to be around humans and all the other fae."

Rowan watches the way Serena's eyes light up as she tells Baba all of this. He smiles to himself, as he too remembers the queen becoming angry over Serena sneaking off to the human world. She would forbid Serena to return there and then take her powers from her for a short time.

Becoming silent for just a moment Serena remembers her youth and smiles at Baba. "She banished Kieran from her presence, and he was forced to live among the humans for a while. He has always hated humans; he views you as insects in comparison to the fae." She picks up a mug of tea and takes a drink, the warm liquid soothing her. Continuing, she says, "Being forced to live among the humans was a humiliating punishment to him. So he ruled over them as a god, treating them cruelly for a few hundred years until my mother could not take his cruelty any longer. She herself has no great love for humans, but she does not believe in treating anyone or anything with such cruelty. She threatened to strip him of all his magic and make him mortal if he didn't stop.

"Kieran, in a fit of fury, rebelled and swore vengeance against my mother. He then created his own realm, a place that is dark and cold to match his heart, a place where only a glimpse of the sun can be seen at any given time. The sky is a constant sea of dark swirling storm clouds, and their acid rain leaves noxious pools of acid spewing foul odors. It is a land broken and bare, riddled with disease and pestilence, a place where every evil being that walks, crawls, flies, or slithers can scratch out its own space among its own kind, content for a time to live in misery because it isn't alone in its suffering." Just thinking about it causes a shiver to pass through her.

"He calls his kingdom Darkheart. His castle floats high above the land, away from the stench and the cries and bickering of those that have chosen to live there."

"Can't they just leave that terrible place once they find out how bad it is?" Baba asks.

"No, he does not allow that! You must understand—he is very charming when he wants to be, but he is also very cruel and hateful!" the princess replies.

"That was when our courts became divided. Separating into the queen's court of light, known to us as the Seelie Court, and Kieran's court of darkness, known as the Unseelie Court. For the most part the fairies of the Seelie Court use their magic for good, for the betterment of our world and all that is in it. All fairies in my mother's court are very powerful and some very dangerous, and a few of those do not like humans at all. Some fairies occasionally play what they consider harmless tricks on humans, my mother's jester for one, but he is another story altogether. They think my queen mother doesn't know what they do. But she does; she just chooses to ignore it so long as no one gets hurt. This is how humans know of our existence.

"The dark fairies who choose to follow Kieran and live with him in the Unseelie Court have always used their magic in very bad ways. They enjoy making humans and the other types of fairy folk suffer. They cause destruction and plague to rain down around them for their own twisted amusement.

"Of course all of this took place many millennia ago, and my mother had not heard so much as a peep from him until our twins were born. The fact that he had demanded that one of the girls be brought to him did not surprise my mother; she had expected as much. Once he had sensed that one of our daughters had perished, due to the spells my mother cast, he seemed to just accept the loss and he left us alone with our grief and our one remaining daughter."

Baba suddenly feels very small and powerless in comparison to these magnificent beings. The story of their past and all the information about Sadie was making her very nervous and afraid, and she thinks, *What if these fairy people decided to keep Sadie? Would I be able to stop them? I love Sadie so much, and I can't even begin to think of what life would be like without her.*

Princess Serena and Rowan explain gently, "It is not our intention to take Sadie away from you. She is still very young and must be protected from Kieran."

"Maybe not you, but what about Kieran? Can you stop him from taking her?"

After talking with Serena and Rowan, Baba is able to calm down a little bit. However, she won't feel completely at peace until both Sadie and she are home safe and sound. Even then she isn't exactly sure how safe she will feel ever again.

As the girls sit quietly playing with Lila's toys, some of them, really strange, miniature people and beasts, come to life and do what the girls tell them to do. At one point the girls are playing with a small unicorn, taking turns flying around the room on its back. Baba began to feel an odd mix of feelings begin to take root in her heart.

"Sadie seems to have taken everything quite well," she says, as a strong need to be home grips her. "I had not planned on being gone this long. I think it's time to leave."

Knowing the thoughts racing through Baba's mind, Serena says, "We understand, and please do not worry so. We have no intention of stopping you from leaving with Sadie. Everything will work itself out over time, and the best place for Sadie right now is in the human world with you, protected by the spells that were cast by my mother when she hid her there."

A feeling of deep relief washes over Baba, "I'm grateful for your understanding and your kindness. I know this must be hard on the both of you as well. I'm sure this has been quite a shock to you."

Turning toward the girls, Baba says, "It's time to go, Sadie. Papa must be wondering where we are by now."

The girls, not wanting to separate but resigned to the fact that for now it can't be helped, hug each other. While hugging Sadie, Lila slips a golden necklace into her hand. Sadie looks at it and sees that attached to the necklace is a crystal in the same shade of periwinkle as their eyes.

"My favorite one," Lila whispers. "Whenever you want to contact me all you have to do is hold the rock to your heart and think of me. This way I will be able to find you even though grandmother has blocked all other kinds of magic. It's because the rock is my favorite that the magic is able to break through grandmother's spell. Personal objects infused with magic and given to others out of love are the most powerful tokens of all."

As she gets ready to leave, Sadie slips the necklace over her head so that the rock rests against her heart.

# DAGHAN

Just as they were about to leave, Queen Aurelia appears and says, "Serena, Kieran is aware that Sadie is alive, and he knows she is here in Fairywinkle with you. He is sealing all the portals so that she won't be able to leave."

"Can't you just unseal them?" Sadie asks.

"Yes, but it will take too long, my sweet," Aurelia replies. "There will only be one place left where a portal can be opened without him knowing. It is at the top of Mystic Mountain behind the great waterfall; he does not know of this place. The journey to get there is a hard and treacherous one. You will need to travel through the Nocturnal Forest at night, and you must not use any magic to aid your travels. We must hurry, as I have no doubt that he is already making arrangements to come for Sadie."

As she turns to speak with her daughter, she sees Mr. Frog sitting quietly in a corner watching all that is happening. He had spent the day lazily roaming the gardens looking for fat juicy bugs, which always seem to taste better here, and relaxing in a fountain or two. He had just come inside to see what was going on because it was growing late in the day.

The queen points at him. "You! This is all your fault! You brought Sadie back here, without permission, exposing her and everyone else to the danger of Kieran's ire. The spells I wove to protect her only work so long as she stays within the human world." Angry, a war waging behind her stormy eyes, she flicks her wrist and Mr. Frog vanishes.

Sadie gasps, clamping her hand over her mouth. Wide-eyed, she wonders what happened to Mr. Frog. She begins to ask but being a little frightened decides to remain quiet.

Queen Aurelia turns toward everyone in the room, her displeasure evident in the fiery flash of her eyes and the tension throughout her body, and takes a deep breath to calm herself. Closing her eyes and clearing her mind, she summons Daghan.

He appears instantly, kneeling before her on one knee, head lowered in respect. Without looking up he says, "My queen, how may I be of service?" His voice has an odd timbre, silky, deep, and somewhat hypnotic.

The queen, always impressed with her favorite warrior, smiles. Daghan senses her approval and stands, and as he does so all eyes turn to him—all eyes except Rowan's.

He is a formidable sight, an arachnid fairy, tall and lean with long powerful limbs. His broad chest and shoulders are wrapped in thick muscle that ripples and flows along his body as he moves. His features are handsome but alien, with slightly large reddish gold eyes. He has pointy ears and high cheekbones, and his nose is straight with a slight flair at the nostrils. His mouth is a little wider than normal with full lips. A strong jaw line and slight cleft in his chin finish off his rakish good looks.

Lila giggles softly and tells Sadie silently, "He has large retractable fangs in his mouth. I think he is the most perfect of all grandmother's warriors."

Hearing Lila giggle, he looks in her direction, giving her a wink and a secret smile. Princess Serena, not missing the exchange between the two, smiles to herself, thinking that he is such a rogue. Serena once had a crush on him herself like most of the female fairies throughout Otherworld.

Rowan, watching the exchange between the three of them, is not impressed. He crosses his arms over his broad chest and glares at Daghan.

Daghan's neck, like the rest of his body, is corded with thick muscle. His skin is golden brown, the hair on his head black and spiky. His warrior's outfit displays the colors of his people, forest green with black webbing shot through it, allowing him to blend in with his surroundings while in the forest.

"I have a quest for you, my loyal friend," Queen Aurelia tells him. "I need you to take my granddaughter and the human female back to their world. Kieran has sensed she is here and is sealing all the portals and making ready to come for her." Smiling a mirthless smile, she looks at Daghan in a conspiratorial manner and says, "I need you to make sure they return home safely. I also ask that you stay with her in the human world. She will need both you and Raine to keep her safe and train her. Over the millennia you have served me well, and you are my most trusted and loyal warrior, so I place her in your charge, knowing that you will guard her with your life if necessary."

Daghan, looking into his queen's eyes and seeing her distress, nods his head in acceptance.

Walking over to Sadie and taking hold of her hands, the queen says, "I know you don't know me, but I am your grandmother, queen of all the fae. I have kept an eye on you, little one, watching you grow these past few years. It pleases me greatly that you finally know the truth about your heritage, and I am sorry that you and Lila must part again, but it is for your own safety and cannot be helped." Aurelia then passes all the love that she is feeling to Sadie silently. "You know, your aunt Alece is really a fairy just like you. Her real name is Raine. I sent her to live with you and keep you safe. She tells me that you can be quite the naughty imp at times!" The queen says this with a grin on her face as she winks at Sadie in understanding.

"Even when you are away from the care of your grandparents Raine is watching over you." Taking both girls into her arms and holding them close, she says, "I promise you both that all will be well. Trust me in this." Kissing their foreheads, she casts a spell of protection around them both and they feel a tickling sensation pass through their bodies. Then she is gone in a twinkling of lights.

Daghan, knowing that there is no time to waste, says, "It's time to leave. We have to make our way without using any magic, so we must hurry—it will be dark soon. The forest is not safe at night in the best of times, and this is not the best of times, I assure you."

Saying their good-byes quickly, the three of them slip out the back way to avoid the possibility of being seen. Daghan, leading the way, ushers Sadie and Baba along at a quick pace. He senses that they are already emotionally and physically exhausted but knows that he has no choice because they all have a very long way to travel and not very much time to do it.

If you had happened to be in the human world in the forest at the lake right about this time, you would have been amazed at what you saw. The sky opens with a loud *boom* as a very large, very green frog drops from above screaming as he splashes down into the middle of his lake. As his head breaks the surface of the water, he sputters, "Well, that was rude! Very rude indeed!" Looking around, he swims to the edge of the lake and hops out. "Oh my, oh my! I must get back! I must help Sadie and Baba. They are in grave danger, and it is all my fault!" Ringing his hands nervously, he mutters, "But how? That's the question! How?"

As they enter Nocturnal Forest the air is cool and sweet smelling, and even though Sadie is a little scared she feels a pulse of excitement hum through her as she struggles to keep up. The pace Daghan sets is quick and steady, not the leisurely walk that she is used to, so it doesn't take long before she starts to tire and begins to lag behind. The muscles in her legs burn because of the steep upward climb. As Sadie grabs ahold of a root to pull herself upward something scratches her hand, "Ouch!" She snatches her hand away, almost losing her balance as she grabs hold of a tree sapling next to her. Looking at the ground, she becomes a little concerned. She would swear that there is something under the dirt with claws trying to grab ahold of her hand.

A little out of breath, she huffs and puffs, talking to herself as she resumes climbing. *Don't be silly, Sadie. It's just your imagination. It was probably just a stick or some pine needles scratching and poking your hands. Nothing from under the ground is trying to grab you.* But she continues to eye the ground warily.

She remembers what Daghan said about the forest before they left the house: "It's not safe at the best of times, and this is not the best of times!" Not really wanting to know what he meant by that, she quickens her pace, squealing every once in a while when she feels something sharp or slimy touch her.

Baba waits for Sadie to catch up, and grabbing hold of her hand she pulls her up alongside herself, trying to help her as best she can even though the climb upward is very steep; she is having a hard time herself. Quietly, she calls to Daghan, "Can we rest for just a few minutes?"

With time quickly slipping by, he watches the sun sink below the tops of the trees, its golden rays flashing between the tree trunks, casting long eerie shadows. Daghan is in a hurry to make it to the falls as quickly as possible, as he knows that once the sun goes down the forest will wake up. Looking at the two females he is sure that they will not be able to continue at the present pace. Resigned to the fact that this journey is going to take longer than he wants it to, he stops and allows the females to rest for a short while.

Climbing a tree so that he will have a better view of the surrounding area, he looks down at the females on the ground and calls out, "I suggest you both climb a tree as well."

Sadie finds a tree with some low branches and quickly climbs it with Baba right behind her. Sadie collapses immediately, her back against the trunk of the tree and her legs hanging off both sides of the branch. She doesn't think there has ever been a time when she has been this tired. The excitement she felt when they first started out is gone; all that is left is an overwhelming need to be home and in her own bed.

Baba can see that the trip so far has already taken its toll on Sadie. She takes the branch just below Sadie's, and leaning back she rests her head against the tree trunk. Gathering her little granddaughter in her arms as best she can, she kisses the top of her head.

"Saaadieee ..." A soft whisper blows through the trees all around them.

Sadie stiffens. "Did you hear that, Baba?" she whispers in her ear.

Baba looks around, listening, and then shakes her head, mouthing silently, *no*.

Sadie scans the forest suspiciously before laying her head back down on Baba's shoulder. She knows that she heard someone whisper her name.

Daghan looks down on them and wonders if the child will have the strength to complete the climb.

Looking at her he thinks, *All this time*! Like everyone else he thought the child was dead. He wonders at what lengths Kieran will go to get to her. It would be a lot easier to use his magic, but he knows that Kieran will be able to locate them if he does. The last thing he needs is Kieran sending something from his realm to intercept them. He has always enjoyed a good fight, but he has no idea what Kieran will send or how many, and he is sure that it will be something particularly evil and nasty because he is very angry right now.

Settling himself on his branch in the tree, he surveys the surrounding area. The rays from the sun have diminished to almost nothing, and darkness is fast consuming the forest. He is able to see very well in the dark. He actually prefers the darkness, because being an arachnid fairy, his vision is better in the dark than that of any other type of fae. In most forests darkness would certainly give them a better chance to pass through unnoticed, but this one isn't like most forests. He continues to search the surrounding area. He knows that this forest holds many secrets, and he is in no hurry to discover what those secrets might be. The mountain was not named Mystic Mountain for no reason. Deep in his own thoughts, he still doesn't miss the slight shift in the forest's energy. His skin tingles in warning: something is coming, and it is coming for them.

Silently dropping down out of the tree, Daghan walks over to where the females are resting so they can hear him when he whispers, "Be as quiet as possible climbing down out of the tree. You need to follow me very quickly and as quietly as possible." The look on his face tells them that their situation has changed and not for the better.

Suddenly feeling more scared than tired, Sadie follows Daghan and Baba through the woods to a maze of tall crinkleberry bushes. It's so big that Sadie and Baba would most certainly get lost in it if left on their own. As Daghan leads them into the middle Sadie's skin tingles as she looks around, and she is surprised at how well she can see. "Saaadieee ..." the melodic high-pitched voice softly calls to her again. She's positive she heard it that time, and she looks from Baba to Daghan. Neither of them seemed to have heard it.

Daghan has them sit down, saying, "I will be back for you when it is safe. Under no circumstances are either of you to leave these bushes until I come back to get you."

Sadie and Baba both look up at him. Sadie can see him perfectly, but Baba can barely see him at all in the darkness. Nodding their heads in agreement they try their best to get comfortable. Sadie gets another tingly feeling. "Saaadieee ..." the ghostly voice calls to her in a whisper that apparently only she can hear. She looks first one way and then the other down both lengths of the thicket. Satisfied that they're alone she snuggles into Baba. *Maybe it's Lila?* she thinks; she hopes.

Baba takes Sadie into her arms again and hopes that it will comfort her in some small way. That's when she realizes that every time she touches Sadie she can see perfectly in the darkness. Thinking about it, she wonders if by touching Sadie, somehow her magic allows her to see as well. She senses Sadie's nervousness and figures it's because they're in a strange place in the dark.

As Daghan leaves he tries to decide if the decision to not use any magic is truly the smart way to handle this mess.

# ELVES

Earlier that same evening in the little village, an elf named Asher, always being on the lookout for something he might miss, sees the two female strangers from earlier that day leaving Princess Serena's house the back way just before dusk. They're following a tall dark figure that he does not recognize. Asher, not being someone to miss out on anything, squats down behind some bushes and calls for his two brothers. "Finn! Bohdi! Come here! You have to see this!" he calls in a thick Scottish brogue. "There's somethin' strange goin' on around here tonight!"

Finn is the first to arrive. He's the middle brother, Asher being the oldest and Bohdi the youngest of the three. The elf brothers have been on their own for a number of years.

Asher has a more serious nature than the other two. Average in height for an elf, he stands about five feet tall. He always dresses the same, being very picky about his appearance, in tight trousers with knee-high cuffed boots, a billowy white shirt, and a leather duster. His shaggy, sandy blonde hair just touches the collar of his shirt. He looks like a cross between a pirate and a cowboy, except that he isn't particularly fond of hats. He feels that they always blow off his head at the wrong times. He has the ability to make himself invisible and then transport to another location. When needed, Asher's weapon of choice is a larger powerful block hammer with a spike on one end.

Finn is the opposite of Asher. He doesn't have a serious bone in his body. He is quick to laugh and very playful. He's also much bigger than Asher, reaching the lofty height of five and a half feet tall, and is much more muscular. His sandy blonde hair is cut shorter and sticks out in all directions. He worships the ground his older brother walks on and likes to dress exactly like him. He has a chameleon-like ability whereby his clothes and skin can change to blend in with his surroundings, basically rendering him invisible. A pair of short swords are his weapons of choice, which he carries crisscrossed on his back for easy access.

Bohdi is a blend of serious and playful with a dash of grumpy. He is usually the smallest of the three, but no one really knows his true height except Bohdi. He has the ability to shrink or enlarge himself at will, which he does quite frequently. Even though he is the youngest, more often than not he acts like a grumpy old Scotsman. He likes to be mysterious and pretend that he is a spy in the service of his queen. Unlike his brothers, he doesn't like to wear long or loose-fitting clothes. He prefers comfortable snug-fitting trousers and shirts and a warm well-tailored coat, all in dark colors, with knee-high cuffed boots. Also unlike his brothers, his hair is long and blond, reaching halfway down his back, and he keeps it braided or tied back in a ponytail.

Princess Serena allowed the brothers to join her troop when she decided to stay in what Asher calls "their forest." She gave them a home of their own and has provided for them ever since, and they repay her kindness by tending the gardens in their small village. They also feel that it's their responsibility to keep an eye out for any mischief that might be happening near the village or in the forest.

Asher quietly calls for Bohdi again, "You'd better hurry or we'll leave you behind!" Asher has decided to follow the three strangers.

Bohdi comes up behind them and wipes his nose on his shirt-sleeve, asking, "What is goin' on?" in his normally loud voice.

Asher shushes Bohdi, saying, "Get down and whisper! Haven't I told you before that you canna be a spy if you're always bein' loud?"

"Ah chew!" Bohdi sneezes.

Asher and Finn quickly jump to their feet, nervously looking around and patting themselves down, having forgotten the strangers in their panic.

Asher, looking down at himself, says, "Aw Bohdi, for the love of magic, that accursed nose of yours has dressed me up all girly-like. Just look at me, poufy yellow pants and curly-toed shoes to match!"

Bohdi sniffs. "Sorry!" he snarks. "You know I canna help it," he says as he squats down, hiding the smirk on his face.

Looking around again to make absolutely sure no one else is out and about, Asher says, "Now I'll have to go and change before we can leave."

Finn smiles. He's glad that it wasn't him this time, and he squats back down beside Bohdi as Asher stomps off to change his clothes.

"The strangers will have a nice head start by the time Asher gets back," Finn says.

"We best call our pets and be ready when he gets here," Bohdi says. Concentrating, they summon their pets.

A fae's pet is made of pure magic, and they only exist when their owners call for them. Most fae have pets of some kind; the kind of pet depends on the fae.

Asher's pet is a big, fierce-looking brown bear named Arlo. Finn's pet is a mean-tempered wolverine named Ryder, and Bohdi's pet is a beautiful, larger-than-normal, blue-eyed snowy owl named Hooty, also known as Grumpy Owl, which suits Bohdi perfectly.

Together the six of them can handle pretty much anything they might find themselves involved in while traveling through the forest at night. Elves may have limited magic compared to royal fairies, but they make up for it with keen sharp minds, a fearless attitude, and a lot of determination. The three brothers have lived in this forest their whole lives, and they know what's out there at night. They also know how to travel without being bothered by what will wake in the forest this night.

Asher returns, already riding Arlo, and calls out, "Mount up. We have wasted enough daylight!"

Asher and Finn take off at a fast pace, while Bohdi takes flight on the back of his owl. Soaring high above the forest, he knows that it's his job to keep an eye on the strangers as his brothers make their way on the ground. It's Finn's job to take the lead and keep an eye on Bohdi's position in the sky. The brothers have developed specific calls that they can use to talk to each other. Anyone listening will think that it's just animal chatter.

Asher feels best when hanging back so he can keep a watchful eye on everything, including his brothers. They are his responsibility, and he takes his responsibilities very seriously. As a family unit they each know their place in the pecking order. They know their strengths and abilities, and together they are usually able to achieve their goals in an orderly and timely fashion. Everyone knows that elves thrive with order, that if you want something done right the first time and without problems, you have elves do it for you.

Bohdi, flying overhead, has found the strangers and is tracking them as they make their way through the forest. It surprises him to see them climbing at such a quick pace, and he wonders what they are up to. He signals his brothers on the ground to let them know that he has an eye on the strangers. Looking up, both brothers notice his position in the sky and realize that the strangers are heading toward the top of the mountain.

Asher wonders where they could be going at this time of the day. He signals to Finn to start climbing upward. He wants to get close enough to see who the dark stranger is so he can try to figure out why they are sneaking around and climbing his mountain so late in the day. Nobody in their right mind would climb this mountain at night! Nocturnal Forest is fine during the day, but at night? No, this makes no sense.

Asher knows that he could just go and ask the princess what is going on, but what would be the fun in that? It's been a very long time since anything really interesting has happened around these parts, and being honest with himself, he wants a little adventure, something to get the old blood pumping. So with a smile on his face and a gleam in his eyes he leans forward and pats Arlo on his neck, feeling good about his decision.

Daghan senses the elves getting closer, and he sniffs the air trying to catch their scent. He can feel their magic—subtle, not strong like it would be if they meant to attack. He relaxes just slightly, knowing that whoever they are, they have not been sent by Kieran. However, that doesn't mean they are friendly!

Having climbed a tree after leaving the females he looks around and notices a white owl soaring overhead. Already having sensed the two on the ground he is sure that this one makes three. "Not so bad, Daghan ol' boy; you've been in worse situations." With the females safely hidden away, he drops to a lower branch and gets comfortable. He wants to see what their next move will be now that their lookout can't see any of them anymore.

Above, Bohdi alerts his brothers that he has lost sight of the strangers. He circles above their last location. He's pretty sure that two of them are in the dense thicket of bushes just a few yards away. "Hmm. Not a very safe place to be at night in this forest." But he has no idea where the third stranger went. He signals his brothers to approach with caution.

Inside the thicket, Sadie has fallen asleep in Baba's arms. Being grateful for the chance to rest but itching to know what is going on, Baba finds it hard to totally relax. Leaning her head back against a thick branch and closing her eyes she takes a few deep breaths. She thinks about all that has happened today and wonders what could be happening with Daghan right now; it all just seems to be a dream.

The fairy folk being real and Sadie being one of them? It's just mind boggling. She hopes that Papa isn't worried sick about them, but she knows that he is. She wonders if he's searching for them, if he's called Alece and the sheriff. This has all just turned into such a mess, one of Sadie's grand adventures to be sure, but a really messy one.

As she relaxes, her mind starts to drift as if floating. She's been so worried about Sadie and all that's come to light today that she hasn't realized how terribly exhausted she is. Laying her cheek on the top of Sadie's head, she snuggles down closer and quickly falls asleep.

Without the use of magic Daghan has to rely on his more basic senses, which he feels are greatly limited when compared to using the magic that comes more naturally to all fae. He concentrates on the approach of what he now knows to be three elves and their pets. Focusing his concentration on the two approaching elves, he doesn't realize that a more serious threat is just a short distance away in the opposite direction.


Inside a cave, the entrance hidden by the large boulders, trees, and bushes that surround it, live two haggard crones, Ezra and Zara, known by all as the demoted ones. They were cast into exile by Queen Aurelia, most of their magic stripped away for repeatedly disobeying her laws concerning the ingestion of the yellow spotted toadstool and crinkleberries.

All fairies are forbidden to eat both of these because of the bad side effects they produce. The toadstools make fairies see and hear things that are not really there. The crinkleberries make them lose control of their powers. Taking just one of these is bad enough, but when taken together it's a bad thing, very bad.

Having only enough magic to barely survive but not enough to keep them healthy and vibrant, their looks have declined over the years. They have lost their beauty and strong forms, becoming ugly, hunched crones, their skin wrinkled and sagging, to all that see them except each other. Their minds are twisted into believing that they still look beautiful, their bodies firm and strong.

The two fashioned their cave into a cozy little home as best they could, angry at the queen for their punishments of being exiled and the loss of most of their powers. They now serve King Kieran, mixing different kinds of potions out of the berries and toadstools for his many uses. Over the years they have both become skilled botanists as well as learning some chemistry, and in exchange for their services, the king has been slowly infusing them with more magic, increasing their powers little by little.

The king knows that their minds are twisted from eating the toadstools and berries, so he is careful not to give them too much magic but just enough to keep them in line and happy. He feels that soon Ezra and Zara will be a force to be feared by all but him. He views them as his secret weapon in his war against Queen Aurelia. The fools feel honored to play what they think is such an important role in his plan to take down the queen. They don't realize that he views them as expendable if necessary. They have fooled themselves into thinking that he feels a kinship with them because of their forced exile. The king doesn't care what the two fools think as long as they keep producing new and improved potions for him to use. He couldn't care less about their fantasies.

Ezra is the first to feel a change in the forest's energy. The two friends have been busy concentrating on combining new ingredients to form a new, particularly nasty potion for their king. Zara looks up from the task she has been working on and asks, "Do you feel that?"

They both tilt their heads back slightly, turning this way and that and sniffing the air. "Yes, I think we have company," Ezra says, a wicked smile forming on her wrinkled face.

They sense the excitement felt by both parties that are wandering into their territory. Drawing on each of their powers and combining them to make them stronger, they send out delicate tendrils of magic to investigate the situation. Like long, thin threads of smoke that slip through the forest unseen, the magic tendrils slither along the forest floor looking for information.

They are careful not to use too much power; they don't want to alert the trespassers to their presence. The information that travels back to them along these tendrils excites them. Together they start gathering potions and other chemicals into their packs. Turning their attention back to the project they had been working on, they hurry to finish it.

"I want it ready when it's time to leave so we can test it on these travelers who have dared to encroach on our home," Ezra tells Zara. They smile at one another in a knowing way, their twisted minds excited by the chance to unleash pain and chaos on their unsuspecting victims.

As Asher and Finn sneak into position on the ground, Bohdi decides to set down on the top of a tree. It just happens to be the same tree Daghan is hiding in. Looking up he knows that the owl and its rider have just landed, but he can't see them from his position in the tree.

Thinking that the owl and its rider are just the lookouts he goes back to searching the ground for the other two. There, just on the other left side of the large thicket that the females are in, he sees a dark figure moving silently through the darkness.

What he doesn't see is the second rider, as Asher and Arlo are invisible. Finn's movements are intended to draw his attention. Even though Asher is invisible that doesn't mean that he can stop the sound of twigs snapping or branches breaking as he and Arlo make their way into position. He could just transport them both into place, but it tends to zap his power for a while, so not knowing if he will need that power to fight he decides that it's better to save it and make his way on foot.

Trying to prepare for whatever is going to happen, Daghan hears a branch snap off to his right. He searches the darkness but doesn't see anything. Snap! There it is again. "Why you wily trickster, You've gone invisible. Nice trick, but you're gonna have to do better than that!" he whispers to himself.

Concentrating, he doesn't expect the high-pitched screech that suddenly splits the air and his eardrums. Unbelievable pain knifes through his head, and pressing his palms against his ears he loses his balance.

Dazed, he slips off his perch in the tree and falls, hitting a branch and bouncing off that one just to hit another. As he's thrown back and forth from one branch to another gravity continues to pull him downward toward the forest floor.

Releasing his head, he tries to grab hold of a branch when another ear-splitting screech fills the air. Missing the branch with his hands, his head slams into it, almost knocking him unconscious. Grabbing his head between his hands again, he tries desperately to block the deafening sound as it echoes through the trees. Barely managing to twist his body around before hitting the ground, he lands in a crouching position, still pressing his hands against his ears.

All at once he sees both elves crash through the tree line and charge him from opposite sides. Watching the two elves race toward him, their pets changing, growing larger with every step, he decides that magic is his only defense. Gathering his powers around him like a cloak, he prepares to defend himself.

His head still ringing, he stands up, feet spread apart, his arms stretched wide with palms up, and tilts his head back as his magic swirls around him. Muscles bunch and twist, expanding and lengthening as his body enlarges. A large pair of white fangs spring out of his open mouth, glistening in the moonlight. An extra set of arms burst from his sides at the bottom of his rib cage. Unable to stifle it, a deep throaty moan escapes past his lips. The extra set of arms grow to their full length within seconds. The hands are clawed with long curved talons designed for slashing and slicing. Twisting and turning his head, his neck lengthens, allowing him better access to sink his fangs deep into his victim's neck.

While the brothers race toward the stranger they see him stand, and they watch in horror as he transforms within seconds. Asher, his eyes glued on the sight before him, suddenly gets a sick feeling inside as he recognizes just who this stranger is. He's heard stories of a great warrior in the service of their queen, undefeated in battle due to his abilities, with a ruthless bloodthirsty nature and a tendency to dispatch his enemies quickly and effortlessly, showing no mercy. It's said that he does it without even breaking a sweat.

Signaling to Finn, the brothers slow their pace and come to a stop just a few feet from Daghan. Fully transformed and ready for battle, he is tense as he waits for the attack.

The brothers' eyes are bulging. With their pets breathing hard, the brothers' strain slightly to bring them under control as they sit atop their mounts. The one sitting on the bear whistles, and soon the owl and its rider swoop down to land on a lower branch just above his head.

The elf on the bear says, "Greetings. My name is Asher. These here are my brothers, Finn and Bohdi." He points from one to the other. "We have been trackin' you since you left our village. We werena really goin' to attack you, we were just havin' ourselves a bit of fun."

"We didna know that we were followin' Daghan, our queen's mightiest warrior!" Finn says in awe.

"We humbly ask your forgiveness for the way we came bustin' out of the forest en all," Asher says as he bows his head out of respect. His brothers, watching closely, copy him and bow their heads as well.

Struggling to compose himself, Daghan realizes that the three elves are no threat to him or the females, and he triggers his transformation back to his normal form. As he does so an idea forms in his mind, a way to transport the females more quickly to the top of the mountain. The three brothers watch his transformation in silence, their mouths hanging open.

He looks from one brother to the next, taking in their demeanor. Relaxing, he leans back against the same tree he had just fallen from a few minutes ago. From the way these three are looking at him, expressions of hero worship written all over their faces, he realizes that stories of his strength and prowess in battle must be circulating throughout the realms, and this pleases him greatly. Crossing his arms over his chest, he absently reaches up and starts to massage his chin with thumb and forefinger, feeling relieved that apparently they did not witness his fall from the tree, because that would be awkward!

He decides to ask the brothers for their help in escorting the females. Looking at Asher, he asks, "Do you speak for your brothers?"

Slightly nodding his head in the affirmative, Asher waits without speaking. He wants to know what is going on and why it would involve the mighty warrior Daghan.

Daghan pushes off the tree to a standing position and, looking Asher directly in the eyes, says, "I have been assigned a very important mission by the queen, and I could use some help if you and your brothers are up for a quest."

Relying on the elves' inquisitive nature, he tells them, "The queen has requested that I escort her granddaughter, Sadie, and a human female back to the human world to protect them from Kieran. I need to reach the falls before he comes for the girl. She has been living with humans all this time to keep her safe. Now Kieran knows that she is alive, and he is coming for her. Will you help her?"

The brothers look at each other, their expressions almost giddy with the aspect of being on a mission with Daghan, and not having any other plans for the night Asher says, "We will. But why the falls?"

"It's the only place left to open a portal." Daghan claps his hands together and, rubbing then back and forth, says, "Great. I'll go and retrieve the females."


After being awakened by an extremely loud screech, Sadie and Baba sit quietly waiting for Daghan to return. Sadie looks around, asking, "Did you hear that, Baba? I thought I heard a scratching sound!"

"I thought I heard something too," Baba whispers.

At first they don't notice the branches around them begin to move. They move slowly, slithering along the ground and across their tops, intending to wrap themselves around Sadie and Baba.

"*Ouch!*" Sadie squeals as she tries to snatch her hand from the ground. "Something's holding my hand, Baba! It won't let go!"

Grabbing hold of her wrist with her other hand, she pulls. Sadie can feel something hanging on to her index finger, its little claws piercing her skin and trying to pull her hand down into the ground. Leaning backward, she pulls as hard as she can until her hand finally pops free. As she raises her hand to her face the sight that greets her eyes is terrifying. Hanging from her finger is a dead squirrel, its little fingers wrapped tightly around hers, its eyes are bulging white orbs. Screaming, she begins shaking her hand up and down and back and forth violently, trying to dislodge it.

"Baba, help me! Get it off me!" she screams.

Baba scoots closer; she can barely see what's happening. She touches Sadie so she can see what's going on. Shocked and sickened at the sight of the decaying squirrel, Sadie starts sweeping her hand in an arc formation back and forth, searching for something she can use to knock it off.

Still shaking her hand as hard as she can, Sadie watches, horrified, as the squirrel's skin begins to slide off its body, revealing slimy muscle tissue and bone. The creature digs its little claws deeper into her skin and tries to sink its teeth into her finger, but its little head keeps snapping back and forth, making it impossible for it to latch on. The putrid smell of the carcass makes Sadie gag as the skin slips completely off, dropping to the ground.

Finally Baba finds a stick. She thinks she can use it to pry the creature off Sadie's finger. She turns back to face Sadie just in time to hear more than see the squirrel go flying into the bushes. Instantly Sadie scoots back in the opposite direction, bumping into Baba.

Turning her head to look at Baba, she cries, "Look out, Baba!" and pushes her out of the way of a long thorny branch that was intending to wrap itself around Baba's neck.

With Baba out of the way the branch snakes down and wraps itself around Sadie's ankle. "*Ouch!*" Sadie wails as it tightens, its thorns digging into her skin as it starts to drag her forward. Already scared from the last attack, this one makes her angry, and she kicks at the branch viciously, shouting, "Get off me! Let go of my leg, you creepy thing!"

The branch begins to wilt. "Get back!" she hollers, putting her hands up as if to block the branches. The branch lets go and instantly retreats, curling back in on itself.

"Okay, that was strange!" Baba says.

"Did you see that?" Sadie exclaims excitedly. "It did what I said! I wish I would have done that with the squirrel. That was so cool!"

"If you say so, munchkin! I could do with less cool things happening, though. Do you think they'll leave us alone now?"

"I don't know, but they sure made me mad. I don't like things hurting you or me!"

Cuddling in close to one another in the middle of the thicket, as far away from the bushes as possible, they resume waiting, both keeping an eye on the bushes and the ground.

While sleeping they didn't notice the two little beetles that crawled out of the ground and up the side of a bush to burrow their way into Sadie and Baba's hair. Attaching themselves to a single strand of hair, a fairies way of tracking someone secretly. Each of the tiny bugs sends a message to their master: "We're ready."

# KING OF DARKNESS

Far away in the distant kingdom of Darkheart, inside his fortress of ebony ice, King Kieran paces back and forth in front of a frosty mirror that hangs on the wall of his private chambers. Turning his face this way and that, he admires the image in the mirror greatly and is proud of the striking male form that gazes back at him. His features are strong and handsome, his eyes so dark they are almost black. Long black hair flows over his strong broad shoulders to the middle of his back. All fae royalty have golden hair and some shade of blue for their eyes. His became dark when he was banished, a testament from the queen proving to one and all that he was no longer royalty. At first he resented this dark look, but with the passage of time he's grown quite fond of it.

"Why Kieran, you look absolutely rakish, a rogue to be sure," he says to his reflection in the mirror smiling. Suddenly his handsome features draw back into a sneer.

"I cannot believe Aurelia lied to me! The sniveling witch stole my heir and hid her from me!" Clenching and unclenching his fists at his sides, he stalks back and forth in front of the mirror. "That fairy witch will pay and pay dearly!" he says, slamming his fist into the open palm of his other hand.

Eyeing himself in the mirror, he raises a single finger and says, "But first I want the child that was rightfully mine to claim." Fuming with anger once again over being so easily fooled, he continues, "Now that I think about it, I never realized how treacherous that witch of a queen could be until now. I have seriously underestimated her, but never again, never again!" he yells. "I will deal with her later!"

Rage fueling his every action, he bellows at the top of his lungs, "*McWeenie!*" The palace shakes as the sound of his voice booms throughout the halls. "McWeenie! Where are you?" Placing his thumb and forefinger on his chin and raising an eyebrow, he says, "I wonder where he goes when he's not attending me. Where could he possibly be that it should take him so long to get here! Come to think of it, I really do not know much about him at all." He waves his hand through the air absently and snorts. "Well, no matter. I'm only interested in the fact that he rarely talks and is always around when I need him, *except for now!*" he screams. "What could be taking him so long?" Gazing at himself in the mirror once again, the king forgets about McWeenie, because all the king truly cares about is himself.

When a small purposeful-looking creature silently appears it takes Kieran a minute before noticing him. Turning around to face the door, he jumps. "Oh, there you are, McWeenie. What took you so long? And do stop sneaking up on me. You know I don't like it!" he snaps. Suddenly the king releases a snort of laughter and then says, "McWeenie? Is that really your family name or was it given to you as a jest sometime in your past and it just stuck?"

McWeenie rolls his eyes and slowly exhales. "My family name to be sure, my lord. You've only asked me that about a thousand times you lack-wit!" he mumbles to himself.

"What? What was that you said, McWeenie? You really must speak up."

"I was commenting on your outfit, sire. I must say, it gives you quite the rakish look."

Kieran continues to inspect himself in the mirror, first presenting his front and then turning to inspect his back, "You do have an eye for fashion, McWeenie. One of your many talents to be sure."

"You flatter me, sire."

He is dressed in snug-fitting black pants, a black shirt with billowed sleeves, and black boots. "I really do look good dressed like a human pirate, don't I?" His eyes roam over his reflection. "Ah yes, those were the days! Remember, McWeenie?" he says with a slight smile that quickly disappears.

"Is all ready for my departure? That witch Aurelia will undoubtedly be trying to sneak the child back into the human world! This cannot be allowed to happen again! Do you understand, McWeenie?"

Nodding in the affirmative and bowing slightly, McWeenie extends his arm in the direction of the door, and to make sure he doesn't make eye contact with Kieran he bows his head as if to say, "After you, my lord." He has been with him long enough to know that he should stop speaking when Kieran switches gears in the middle of a conversation. It would only lead to making him angrier than he already is, and not wanting to be the victim of that anger, he remains silent.

Kieran sweeps past him with an air of haughtiness, dismissing him without a second thought.

Ancient eyes follow him as he leaves the room. McWeenie's lips curl into a sly smile as he follows the strutting peacock out of the room, and he begins whistling a long forgotten tune as he disappears behind Kieran.

Kieran turns and looks around, musing, "What is that tune that he's always whistling? I have never heard such a tune anywhere before except from him. Hmm."


Daghan enters the thicket where he left the females to find them already standing, stretching their arms and legs. Sadie's head snaps up when she sees him.

"Daghan, you missed it! We were sitting on the ground waiting for you to come back when all of a sudden a dead squirrel grabbed my hand and tried to pull it under the ground. I had to shake my hand really hard to keep it from biting me. Then the branches reached out and tried to grab Baba, but I pushed her out of the way and it grabbed me instead. It grabbed ahold of my ankle, and that hurt pretty bad cuz of its thorns. Anyway, the really cool part is that I yelled at them to get away and they did! One even wilted and died! Isn't that cool?"

Daghan is both proud and amazed for some reason. "Well done, Princess. Being scared must have caused your magic to awaken."

Sadie beams at his high praise and says, "It happened when I got mad, Daghan, not when I was scared."

"Really, when you got mad? Well, whatever brings it out is your tell. By the way, I've run into the elf brothers from the village, and they will be joining us on our journey to the top of the mountain."

As they leave the thicket Sadie says, "Wait!" and stops and listens. "I don't hear any of the normal noises we should hear in a forest, Baba. It's so quiet!" Looking around, she says, "No owls hooting, no squirrels scampering, no crickets chirping, nothing! The forest is spooky quiet! Don't you think so too?"

Rubbing her hands up and down her arms, not because she's cold but because she has a really creepy feeling, she says, "Daghan, I keep getting this feeling that there's something out there watching me, and I keep hearing something whispering my name—Saadiee— like that. Something is out there following me, Daghan, waiting for me!"

"Waiting for you? Why?"

"I don't know; it's just a feeling."

"This forest can be very creepy. Try not to let it scare you too much, okay? All is well, and besides, with your new powers I'm quite sure you have nothing to worry about."

Not convinced, she looks around, and suddenly Lila enters her mind. "Be strong, Sadie, you're not alone," she feels her say, and it helps a little bit. But now she knows that the ghostly whispering isn't Lila calling to her.

As they get closer to where the elves are waiting, Sadie sees the animals first. "Those animals look awfully scary, but the elves are absolutely adorable! They're all different sizes. The one on the bear is about your size, Baba. Look, they all have scruffy hair, and their ears are pointy like the fairies." Whispering, she asks, "What's that mean-looking hairy thing with really big teeth that the biggest elf is sitting on, Baba?"

"It's a wolverine, I think. I didn't know they got that big!"

"Hey, those are the same elves we saw in the village today. Look at the tiny cute one sitting on an owl's back, Baba."

"Oh, he keeps sniffing and wipes his little nose on his shirt-sleeve every so often," Baba says.

Sadie finds them fascinating as one by one they introduce themselves.

"Why do they talk like that, Baba?"

"They have what is called a Scottish brogue, Sadie. I like it!"

Daghan tells Sadie and Baba, "The two of you will be riding with Asher and Finn on the backs of their pets. The animals will grow to accommodate your size and weight," he says, misreading the looks on their faces.

Feeling a little apprehensive about the animals but happy to ride so they don't have to walk, they climb up onto the animal's backs and settle themselves behind the elves.

Sadie reaches up absently and scratches her head, and as she does so she notices that Baba is doing the same. The little beetles hold on tightly.

As they all start to climb the mountain again, Sadie feels a slight tug at the back of her mind like a memory that you just can't quite grab ahold of. Something she's forgetting? She tries to shake the feeling but doesn't quite manage to do so, and she looks around, straining her eyes to see as far as she can. She blinks, a little startled, because she's positive she saw something this time, a shadow of what looked like a big dog. Scratching her head again, she turns her attention to Finn.

As the rest of his troop starts off once again up the side of the mountain, Bohdi and his owl prepare to take off again.

"Aw chew!" Bohdi sneezes again. Peals of laughter ring through the forest from Sadie, and the others turn to see what she is laughing about. They find Sadie and Finn sitting on the ground, their legs stretched out in front of them, and sitting between Finn's legs is a squirrel.

"Aw Bohdi," Finn says. "Ryder ain't gonna like this at all! Not at all! He has a bad enough temper without you addin' this to it! For the love of magic, Bohdi, would you just look at the expression on his wee little face?"

Looking at the squirrel, Bohdi gulps and eyes it nervously, saying, "Well, I best be off then. Sorry, Ryder. I really am!" In a hurry to be gone he gives a swift yank on his owl's feathers. She responds by biting his foot as she jumps off the branch. The last thing they hear is Bodhi yelping and then cursing his owl. "Ouch! Blasted, wretched owl, why'd you go and bite my foot? You crazy bird!"

Finn reaches out to pet the squirrel, and it tries to bite him. Yanking his hand back, he says, "Hey now, it isna my fault! So be nice!"

Sadie starts laughing again as the squirrel hangs its head and makes a puffing sound. Giving everyone a surly look, Ryder turns and starts to climb up onto Finn's shoulder.

"Oh no you don't!" Finn says, grabbing ahold of Ryder by the scruff of his neck and gently putting him back on the ground. "If you were to change back while ridin' on my shoulder you'd break my back!"

Resigned to his fate, Ryder hangs his head and starts slowly walking upward, his tail dragging along the ground behind him.

As the three of them start off on foot, Finn drags his hand across his face, mumbling, "I have the feelin' that this is gonna be a vera long night!"

Daghan turns to Asher, grinning, and asks, "What is that all about?"

In reply Asher smiles and says, "When Bohdi sneezes, crazy things happen! We have tried, but there isna a way of stoppin' it."

Daghan shakes his head, saying, "Can't he just change Ryder back?"

"Nope, it has to wear off all on its own. And there's no tellin' how long it will take."

"Great, just great, as if this forest wasn't strange enough. Come on. We'd better catch up."

Looking down, Bohdi keeps a sharp eye on those climbing the mountain. He decides to circle out a little wider, searching for anything out of the ordinary. To his surprise it doesn't take him long to catch sight of two dark patches moving in a diagonal path up the mountainside. Whatever that is, it seems to be moving in the same direction as his troop. He is not too worried, because the distance between the two dark things and his troop is quite a stretch. He decides to keep an eye on them anyway, just to see if they stay their course or change directions.

Continuing to search the mountainside, he circles higher in order to keep an eye on both parties at the same time. As he climbs to a greater height he feels the air becoming a bit nippy. Fighting the pull of the wind, he finally manages to get his coat buttoned, and he leans in closer to Hooty for a little warmth, settling in for a more comfortable flight.


Neither of them being able to see well in the dark, the demoted ones make their way upward. Climbing over fallen trees and tripping over what seems to be every root, rock, and low-growing shrub in the forest, they can't help but feel that this bright idea might turn out to be a big mistake.

Wearing dark cloaks, their hoods are pulled up over their heads to hide their faces, making it even harder to see in the suffocating darkness. Ezra and Zara desperately want to catch up to their prey, but they don't want to alert them by using magic to light their path. So they stumble on through the night, groping and feeling their way up the side of the mountain, each quietly cursing a blue streak every time they hit the ground after tripping over something.

# FINN

It actually doesn't take too long for Ryder to change back to his normal surly self.

Sadie, trying to get comfortable, snuggles closer to Finn, and says, "An elf, an actual elf, and I am riding with him on the back of a wolverine that just a short while ago was a squirrel! I can hardly believe it. No one back home will believe this!"

Sadie is feeling much better about the day she's had. Finding out that she is actually a fairy princess explains so much and makes her feel a lot better about herself. She realizes that just maybe life as a fairy might not be so bad, because she is having the best adventure of her life, right now! The fear that she had been overwhelmed by is gone, replaced by the feeling of exhilaration. Looking over at Baba, she realizes that it doesn't look as though she is having as much fun as Sadie being out at night and riding through a strange forest. "This should be a little scary!" she thinks. "But it's not." She feels alive in so many ways that she can't begin to explain.

Tapping Finn on the back, she asks, "Can we go faster so I can feel the wind in my hair?"

"I'd like to grant you your wish, Princess. I surely would, but I canna!" Finn replies.

She wishes she were tiny like Bohdi so she could fly with him on the back of his owl. That thought brings a question to her mind.

Tapping Finn on his back again to get his attention, she asks, "Why is Bohdi so much smaller than you and your brother Asher?"

"Elves are magic too, you know? It's his magic that gives Bohdi the ability to change his size. Some fairy folk can even change inta somethin' completely different than their normal self. Now take Daghan for instance. He looks completely different when he's in battle form, real scary too if you ask me."

"Daghan! He changes? What do you mean he changes?"

"Aaa yes! Well, you know, so he can protect you! Yes that's it, so he can protect you!"

"Oh, okay." Changing the subject back to Bohdi, Sadie asks, "Since Bohdi shrinks himself so that he can fly on the back of his owl, do you think he can shrink me too so that I can go flying with him some time?"

Looking at her, he wonders why she doesn't just shrink herself; after all she's a fairy too. Thinking about it, he decides that maybe she can't because she's been living with humans her whole life. Maybe she doesn't know that the same magic exists inside of her. Not wanting to be the one to talk about it with her, he says, "Sure, I doona see why not. You can ask him yourself when we see him again."

Excited, Sadie can't help but feel that this day just keeps getting better and better. "My life is changing so fast, but in a good way, you know?" She keeps Finn's attention on her by speaking out loud. "What I really want to do is talk to Baba about everything that has been happening to me. When we left home this morning I was hoping for a grand adventure. But never, not even in my wildest dreams, did I think this day would turn out like it has, I just have so many things to talk about with Baba. I hope Papa isn't too worried, but I know he is worried sick with fear because he doesn't know where we are or what is happening to us. Surely by now Papa has called Aunt Alece, or I guess I can call her 'Raine' now. Anyway, I'll bet they're both out looking for us right now."

As Sadie's one-sided conversation drones on and on, Finn can't help but feel that he might go insane if she doesn't stop talking. An idea suddenly pops into his brain. "A sleepin' spell! It wouldna hurt anything if she were to take a wee nap. The more rest the better at her age, I say, and it will keep me from tearin' my own ears off!" he snarks, mumbling.

Sadie, still jibber-jabbering away as if nothing has changed, suddenly starts yawning. She shakes her head as if to shake away her sudden sleepiness and says," "Poor, poor Papa," and that is her last thought before falling sound asleep.

Finn, smiling and feeling quite pleased with himself, looks over his shoulder at the little girl to make sure that she is situated in such a way that she won't fall off while sleeping. As a precaution he magically wraps a sash around both of them to keep her in place. Proud of the fact that he came up with the idea of a sleeping spell and now enjoying the peace and quiet of the forest, he looks over toward his brother and smiles. That's when he notices the stink-eye Asher is sending him, disapproval written all over his face.

Finn glances sheepishly at the human riding behind Asher. She looks lost in her own thoughts and hasn't seemed to notice. Relieved, he looks back at Asher and shrugging his shoulders says in elven, "Better a little disapproval from you than feelin' as if my ears are bleedin' from the little princess's nonstop jibber-jabberin'."

Daghan, not missing the interaction between the brothers but unable to hear what's being said, smiles knowingly as he looks at the expressions on their faces. Having come from a large family himself, he knows what it's like to be on either side of a given situation between siblings. Looking over his shoulder to check on the two females he sees that the small one called Sadie is fast asleep. *That's interesting*, he thinks to himself. *Didn't the older human female tell me they had slept for a time while waiting inside the thicket?* Looking over at her, he sees that she seems oblivious, lost in her personal thoughts. Daghan decides that it's not worth disturbing her.

He watches Asher look up and to the side every so often to check on his brothers, noting that he appears to be an elf of very few words. Riding in silence, he seems to keep a watchful eye on everything and everyone around him.

Daghan can't help but feel that luck was with him when meeting up with the elf brothers. Forging an alliance with them has turned out to be a very good thing. He thinks to himself, *We're making excellent time now and not having to stop for rest periods. Everyone is off the forest floor, and their pets seem to be doing a fine job keeping the nocturnal forest creatures away from the troop.* The pure magic that rolls off a fairy's pet seems to have adverse effects on anything made of dark magic. *They are just what I needed to help me complete this journey.*

*If we can continue to climb at this same pace the troop should reach the falls within the next couple of hours.*

Looking over at Sadie again and watching her sleep so peacefully, snuggled against the elf's back, he can't help but wonder if that stink-eye he saw Asher give Finn didn't have something to do with the little girl falling asleep so suddenly. Chuckling to himself, he thinks back on his own life, remembering his younger siblings. More than once he wove a sleeping spell for them—apparently the very young of all races have a gift for jibber-jabber. Smiling about some far-off memory, he continues to climb.

# SOMETHING WICKED

Farther back down the mountain, Ezra and Zara continue to struggle, desperately trying to catch up with the strange travelers. Muscles and lungs burning, sweat dripping into their eyes, they are both wondering what has possessed them to embark on such a treacherous journey.

The forest has been battling them all night. It took a while, but they finally noticed that they weren't tripping over things but were in fact being tripped by things. "Dead things reaching out of the ground and grabbing our feet, clawing at our legs, trying to trip us. They want to drag us under the ground so they can feed on us!" Ezra says.

"True, the blasted things have been a real pain!" Zara replies.

"Have you noticed that the trees have been moving as well? Their long finger like vines that hang down out of them have been trying to wrap around my neck and arms. Everything in this forest seems to want to feed off of the living, including the dead!" Ezra complains.

"There are things here that will kill us just for the fun of it!" Zara says and shivers.

"Giant fire-spitting toads! I've heard they belch flames and they have these really long tongues that shoot out of their mouths so fast you don't even see them before they grab hold of you. They're tipped with flaming balls of goo that envelope you and slowly dissolve you as they drag you back into their gaping mouths to swallow you whole if their hungry. If not, they just watch you melt!" Ezra says as she looks around. "It's said that the toads can swallow a fully grown male fairy."

Ezra and Zara have never actually seen one of these toads, but they have heard stories about them their whole lives, which is why they usually don't venture out after dark. Testing a new potion on a stranger who just happens to pass by their cozy little home is one thing. But chasing after strangers in the dark and climbing the mountain to do it is madness, even for them.

Due to their limited amount of magic, they are only able to see a little better in the dark than most humans can. Still, they decide not to use their magic to light their path.

Exhausted, Zara plops down on a fallen tree and greedily inhales the sweet-smelling air.

Ezra drops down to sit beside her and breathes in deeply as she pulls her hood back. Enjoying the feel of the night's cool air as it comes into contact with her hot skin, she shrugs out of her cloak. Feeling like it's trying to suffocate her, she tosses it aside with a bit of a temper as she looks through the darkness at her friend. "What are we doing, Zara? Why exactly did we decide to follow these strangers? We've had to practically crawl through this forest! Climbing the side of this stupid mountain in the darkness and we don't even know who it is we are trying to catch up to, and for what, a bit of fun? I begin to see why all the other fae think we are crazy."

Zara, pulls her cloak from around her shoulders and lays it on the tree beside her. She looks over at Ezra. "Do you think I like this any more than you? No, I do not!" Leaning forward, her elbows on her knees, she absently picks at her front teeth. Spitting, she begins to whine, "My hands and knees are bruised and bleeding from the countless times I have fallen on my face because of those nasty dead things. They have been constantly clawing at my feet and cloak all night! I still have some dirt and small bits of flora between my front teeth from that last nasty fall I took." Glancing sideways at Ezra, she continues her tirade, "If you were to take all the times that I have fallen and add them together it would be the same as me sliding halfway down this hideous mountain on my face tonight!" she screeches at the top of her lungs. "I think I swallowed a bug too!" she says, sighing. "And who knows what we have been stepping in?" she shrieks. "For the love of the first one from which we all came, can't we just go home?"

Ezra looks over at her and slowly blows out her a breath, saying, "I think that we need to think about our situation, Zara. I do not feel that it is possible to catch up with them without the use of magic. As we sit here, they are gaining distance on us. Sewell and Belfry are too small to carry us."

"True, but we could make our pets bigger!" Zara says.

"It would take much more power than we have to make a bat and a rat big enough to carry us. We've come too far to turn back now. We have no choice but to use a bit more magic in order to catch up with them."

Zara, knowing that it's futile to argue with Ezra when she is set on achieving one of her goals, gives up and nods her head in agreement and then asks, "Do you think we have enough magic to finish this?"

Ezra smiles, knowing she has won the argument. Smiling in a very wicked way, she grabs Zara's hands to combine their magic. They close their eyes and concentrate, and whispering they begin to chant.

From high above Bohdi can only see that the two dark patches he's been tracking have stopped moving. Nudging his owl they circle back around for a closer look. As he glides through the air circling downward he squints, trying to focus. Dropping closer, Bohdi can see now that the two figures are sitting close together on a fallen tree. Reaching the treetops, he is mildly startled to find that the dark shapes are fae. He frowns, not sure why he suddenly gets a creepy feeling. "I think it would be best if we were to get a closer look, doona you agree, girl?" Hooty picks a lower branch in a tree behind the two figures. Softly, without any noise, she lands. They sit listening for just a minute, shocked at what he hears and sees, and he nudges Hooty to get out of there.

"Hooty, I have a funny feelin' in the pit of my stomach! We need to be gettin' back to the troop! I canna communicate with Asher and Finn from way out here."

Gently he tugs at the feathers on the back of his owl's neck, and she responds by flapping her wings to gain altitude so they can head for the top of the mountain to catch up with his brothers. As they change directions he pushes her to fly faster. He lies flat against his owl's back for greater speed as they soar through the night sky trying to reach his brothers in time. In time for what he doesn't know; he just knows it isn't going to be good.

Increasing their speed and climbing higher, they race toward their destination. Suddenly the wind picks up, becoming more forceful and pushing back at them as they struggle to fly. The wind batters them, forcing them downward. Tightening his hold on Hooty, he says, "Come on, girl. I know you can flap harder." He uses his magic to weave a spell around both of them to keep the wind from dragging them down out of the sky.

Suddenly a bolt of lightning streaks through the air directly above their heads. Bohdi instinctively ducks and yells, "Great thunderbolts of lightning!"

The clap of thunder that follows sends out a shock wave that hits them like an enormous hammer, sending them reeling sideways, spinning round and around out of control. Bohdi hangs on for dear life as he watches the ground get closer and closer. He tries to weave another spell and finds it hard to stay focused as they plummet downward, spiraling toward the trees. As he concentrate harder, the air around them finally starts to twinkle; it sizzles and snaps. Relieved by the feel of his magic, they manage to level out, and for the first time in his life he begins to wonder if traveling by foot isn't a better idea after all.

Swooping low to glide above the treetops, they continue to fly toward the top of the mountain. Looking back over his shoulder, he sees a flash of light illuminate the sky, and he can see that a huge dark mass is forming. The clouds swell to enormous heights as the wind whips at them, making them push and shove against each other, causing the night sky to light up again and again. Jagged bolts of lightning slice through the clouds, splitting apart to form long bony, wicked-looking fingers like that of a witch reaching down from the heavens to score the ground. The thunder is deafening as it rolls through the air in shock waves all around him. Turning around and once again lying flat against his owl's back, he says, "Fly, girl. You must fly faster!"

Arlo and Ryder are the first to notice a shift in the forces of nature that surround them. They stop suddenly. Looking up, they sniff the air, its icy bite making them shiver. This action alerts their masters to the coming storm.

Asher and Finn look skyward for Bohdi's owl. Finn turns to Asher and raises his voice, competing with the howling wind. "Look at the tops of the trees, they're bendin' half way to the ground now! I'm tellin' you—the storm is only gettin' started!"

Asher calls out to Daghan, who is just a little farther ahead, "Look up!"

The brothers spur their pets into action. Asher tells the human woman behind him, "Hang on tighter so Arlo can increase his speed to catch up with Daghan."

Looking up, Daghan wonders where the storm has come from "It seems to have come out of nowhere and without warning," he says in a loud voice as the brothers come up alongside him. "Something magic has come into play now. I think it would be best if we hurry."

# RAINE

Sadie's Papa sits in his empty house worrying. He's already called Alece and the sheriff. Now all he can do is sit and wait for them. At first he wasn't overly concerned; after all it wasn't the first time his wife and granddaughter had lost track of time while out on a walk. But as it got closer to supper time and they still hadn't returned he started calling the neighbors. He thought that maybe they had stopped to visit with one of them on their way home, but no one had seen them. That was when he started to worry. Now he is just plain scared; they have never been gone this long or stayed out this late before. Unable to sit still, he stands up and starts to pace. Back and forth he walks beside the kitchen table. His arms crossed over his chest as he paces, he thinks, *Where could they be?* He stops pacing because he hears a car door slam and then footsteps as they pound up the wooden stairs of the front porch. Alece bursts through the front door as if wild animals are chasing her. "Have you heard anything yet? It's been half an hour since you called to tell me that they weren't back from their walk." Crossing the room in just a couple of strides, she walks into her father's outstretched arms, and as they close around her she feels the first tears slip quietly from her eyes.

The human family that has been raising Sadie, the same family that believes Alece is their daughter, sister, and aunt is unaware that the queen also placed her in their midst to keep watch over Sadie.

Alece is really an elemental fairy, a very powerful being. She has the ability to control the elements. Her skin is normally very light in color with a soft blue glow to it. Tall and slender, her muscles are well defined and sleek. Her given name is Raine. But in order to blend in with the humans she had to change her name and her facial features from their natural appearance. She chose a pretty oval face with big green eyes that are surrounded by thick black lashes, high cheekbones, a small straight nose, and a little mouth with soft full lips. Her real features are only slightly different from what she chose.

In the beginning it was difficult being separated from her home and everything that was familiar to her. Not being able to use her magic was very challenging. But she adapted, and over the years she has grown to love these kind people and at times feel that they are truly her family.

Now, feeling like she has failed her queen and being worried for Sadie and her human mother, she needs to gain control of this situation. Even though Sadie is very powerful and has the ability to control a great amount of magic, she is unaware of this and has never been trained to use it, especially as a defense.

Breaking loose from her human father's vise-like hug, she takes a step back and looks into his eyes. They look haunted with worry and pain. She decides to tell him the truth. "Dad, I need to tell you something. Let's sit at the table." She knows that she must contact the queen immediately and wonders why the queen has not contacted her.

Looking him in the eyes, she says, "First I want to say that I've grown very fond of all of you." He looks at her questioningly. "I know that sounds weird, and I'm sorry, but I'm not really your daughter, and Sadie isn't your granddaughter. We are fae, or as you might call us, fairies."

"What? Why are you saying this? That's ridiculous! I have known you your whole life. You're my daughter! I remember you being born, Alece. Why would you say such a crazy thing?"

"I know it's hard to believe, and I don't have a lot of time to explain, so I will just show you!" She snaps her fingers, and a vase of flowers appears on the table between them. Looking into his eyes, she smiles.

"First a talking frog and now this? What is going on! What's happening?" Trying to get a hold on his emotions, he says, "Okay, okay. So if you're not my daughter and Sadie's not my granddaughter. Who are you and what are you doing here? Why do I have all these memories?"

Reaching out, Alece takes hold of his hand, "I know it's a lot to take in, and I'm sorry I don't have the time it will take to explain everything, but I have to contact my queen right now so I can find out what's going on. Please, just give me a few minutes!"

Summoning her magic, she feels a tingling sensation start to spread throughout her body. The air around her sizzles and snaps. The tingling spreads and becomes more intense as it fills every ounce of her being. It has been so long since she last felt the exhilaration of power pulse through her body with the same rhythm as a heartbeat. She welcomes it like a long-lost friend, and directing the flow of power she begins to reach out with her mind. Searching for her queen, she keeps running into barriers, finding all the portals sealed. It's not in her nature to give up, and she refocuses her energy and tries a different approach. Instead of throwing herself against the barriers, she feels her way around them. She searches for weak spots, places where the magic has thinned, separated, or left some small opening in its energy field. Continuing to search one barrier after another, she finally becomes frustrated, as she has been unable to find even the tiniest crack or hole in any of them. Then she remembers her queen telling her about the portal at the top of the mountain and that she created it in secret when she brought Sadie to the human world. Alece had been instructed to only use it in an extreme emergency. She had forgotten all about it until now.

Searching with her mind she finds the portal and easily slips through. Immediately she is filled with a sense of belonging, and her magic increases to ten times the power of what it was. As the power infuses her body, she pushes her mind outward, pushing at it harder, willing it to slide faster and faster along the intricate web of magic that connects everything in their hidden world. Within seconds she is in Avendale. The power of her queen surrounds her instantly, and she is overwhelmed by her presence. Her mind is flooded with information, her essence bombarded by its urgency. Unable to take it all in, she draws back just a little, giving herself the space she needs to absorb everything that is being pushed on her all at once. Understanding and acceptance flows from Raine to her queen, and in that same instant she is gone, traveling back to the human world and back to her body.

As Alece opens her eyes, her human father is there, looking at her, a strange look in his eyes. She begins flexing her muscles, starting with her hands and moving on to the larger muscle groups. "I had forgotten how strenuous it is to separate my mind from my body. I'm one of a select few who have the ability and the power to achieve mind travel," she says proudly.

"You look a little odd, sweetheart! Are you okay? Maybe you should lie down."

"Dad, I'm fine, really! I only look this way because in order to enter my world I have to change back to my normal self. What you're seeing is a blend of the two because I leave my body here. It'll change back; don't worry."

"What did you find out? Are they okay?"

"I believe they are fine for now, but I must leave right now. I have to get to them."

"Fine for now? What does that mean?"

"Dad, I have no time to explain. You're just gonna have to trust me. I have to leave right now so I can get back to my world where I can protect them."

"Fine. You can explain on the way, because I'm coming with you."

Looking at the expression on his face, she knows it would be pointless to argue. "Fine. Let's go!" Taking hold of her father's hand, she transports them to the falls.

They materialize at the beginning of a narrow ledge that wraps around the cliff and disappears behind the waterfall. Carefully they navigate the thin ledge, sliding their feet along the slippery rock, the ledge only wide enough to fit their toes. They hang on with their fingertips, moving slowly, their bodies pressed tightly to the face of the cliff.

"Can't you just zap us behind the falls? It would be a lot easier!"

"Yes it would be easier, but I can't. I can't see what's behind the waterfall or I would just zap us back there, as you put it."

"Sorry, just asking."

As they make their way behind the wall of water Alece is relieved to find a small ledge to stand on. Turning and facing the backside of the waterfall, she takes hold of her human father's hand. Giving it a squeeze, she asks, "Ready?"

Closing her eyes, she softly chants:

*"As the water flows from the falls,*
*Let one from home break down the walls.*
*Two to pass through this gate.*
*A traveler's woes may be their fate.*
*Enter all with happy hearts,*
*This is where adventure starts!"*

Concentrating, she tries to open the portal, but she can't quite get a hold on it. Something is blocking her from creating the portal, and panic seizes her. Calming herself she tries again—nothing! Not understanding what is happening, she sinks to the floor dejectedly. "Something is terribly wrong! I can't get the portal open."

"Are you sure you can't open it? Is there something you're forgetting? I mean seriously, when was the last time you did this? I'm just saying that maybe you've forgotten something."

Sitting there, she tries to pull herself together so she can think clearly. Her hands fisted, she presses them into her thighs as she says, "I am out of time, and I must find a way in." Feeling helpless and irritated, tears slip quietly from eyes. She dashes them away with the back of her hand, angry at her own weakness.

Her father looks on helplessly.

Taking deep breaths to calm herself, she concentrates. "In my human form I have very limited powers, and you can't enter the hidden world without a silver bough anyway. That's it!" Turning to her father, she says, "A silver bough! We need a silver bough for you, and I need to change into my natural form. You were right—I did forget something. I'll be back in a flash!" Gathering her power, she transports herself to the silver pine as she transforms back into her natural self, an elemental fairy named Raine.

# NO TIME FOR PANIC

Holding on tight to Arlo, Asher tries to keep both the human woman and himself from falling off his back as the bear lopes upward through the darkness, weaving his way through the trees and picking up speed as he goes. Asher keeps looking up, hoping to catch a glimpse of snowy white wings, wondering where Bohdi could be and what could be keeping him away for so long. He figures that it has something to do with the approaching storm, so he tries to stay calm. Panicking because Bohdi has been gone for such a long time will in no way help their situation. It will only serve as a distraction, and he needs to keep his wits about him.

"The last thing Daghan needs on this mission is an elf goin' off all willy-nilly actin' like a ninny over nothin'," Asher mumbles.

"Did you say something?" Baba asks as she hangs on tightly.

"Just talkin' to myself!" he snarks.

"You do that quite a bit, you know."

"I know, I know," he says as he scans the sky again. "I'm just worried about Bohdi."

"Oh! Sorry. I'm sure he's fine. The three of you seem to be very capable."

"Humph!" He looks over at Finn and Ryder. The wolverine is able to keep up with Arlo easily and is even better at weaving through the trees.

At last Asher hears a familiar screech ring through the air, and he relaxes. Looking up, he sees white wings circling overhead. He can tell that the wind is blowing much harder above the tree line than on the ground by the way the owl keeps dipping her wings as they are tossed this way and that. He watches the owl carefully make its way down through the trees, almost hitting one or two of them. The two brothers, having caught up to Daghan, wait patiently for Bohdi to land on a branch.

Looking down and seeing all their questions plainly written across their faces, Bohdi doesn't waste any time. "There are two fae followin' the troop!" he says, showing two fingers. "They started chantin', and even though I couldna hear exactly what was bein' said, I know it was somethin' bad cuz this storm whipped up all of a sudden like after that. So I know it's them that is makin' it! They sent a lightnin' bolt after me en Hooty. It about knocked us out of the sky! I believe they're tryin' to stop us from reachin' the top of this mountain! Aw chew!" He wipes his nose on his shirt-sleeve.

In the midst of all the laughter that breaks loose Daghan thunders, "For the love of the first one, Bohdi! Why can't you control that blasted beak of yours?" Daghan, standing below Bohdi, looks up at him through a mass of kinky, curly hair that has engulfed his head.

Finn is unable to stop laughing, because Daghan's normally short spiky hair is now a mass of long, poufy curls that spring straight up out of his head only to collapse around his face like a giant floppy mushroom. "Not so funny now, is it, Daghan?" Finn asks.

"Not as funny as you sitting astride a squirrel!" Daghan snarks. With a huff he tries to push the hair back out of his face, and that's when he notices his hands. Holding them out in front of himself, he stares at them in disbelief. He turns them front to back repeatedly,

"Look! Just look at my hands! They're the hands of an ogre! Big, hairy, ugly!"

"Your hands? I would be concernin' myself with those feet of yours and those ears! Would you just look at the size of those ears?" Finn says laughing.

"My ears?" Feeling his ears as best he can with his giant hairy hands, "My ears! They're the size of tents!" He says his voice climbing higher. "And my feet! Just look at my feet, they're the size of small toboggans! He squeals shrilly. "By the queen's garters Bohdi! I'm going to strangle you with them!"

"Sorry, Daghan. I didna mean to! Please doona strangle me with Her Majesty's garters!" Bohdi pleads, believing that he would actually do it. As an afterthought he asks, "What exactly are these queen's garters you are goin' on about?"

"Oh! Never mind!" Daghan snarks.

Trying to push the hair out of his face, Daghan gives up and gathers it all together and ties it together sticking straight up off the top of his head. That just brings on another round of laughter. Asher, keeping quiet, is just glad it wasn't his turn again.

Baba is having a great time listening as all the men have a go at each other with insults, and she waits patiently for things to finally quiet down and return to normal business.

Daghan crosses his arms over his chest and begins massaging his chin with his giant thumb and forefinger.

Asher tries very hard not to laugh while Daghan's trying to be serious.

Looking up at Bohdi, Daghan asks, "Did you get close enough to see if these strangers were male or female?"

Bohdi, scrunching up his face as he tries not to laugh, thinks for a moment, "Now that I think about it, it seems to me that they did move around kinda girly-like. And the way that they sounded when they were talkin' did sound girly-like." Looking down at Daghan and the others, he shrugs his shoulders.

Daghan thinks for a minute and then turns to Asher and Finn and asks, "Do the two of you know who they could be? Who lives in this forest who might want to do us harm?"

The three brothers look from one to the other and then all burst into laughter, unable to hold back any longer.

Finn, holding his stomach from laughing so hard says, "We're all real sorry, Daghan!" Wiping a tear from his eye, he continues, "It's just that it's hard to look at you and take you serious, with all that floppy hair on your head stickin' straight up like it is! Not to mention the size of your ears and those big hairy hands! And your feet—you could stomp ol' Kieran into the ground with those things!"

Daghan, not in the mood for any more laughter, smiles at them, showing his fangs as he says very quietly, "Who could they be?"

Seeing his glistening fangs, they remember who they are laughing at, and as a chorus they all say, "The demoted ones!"

Dropping his arms to his sides, Daghan rolls his eyes and looks skyward. Taking a deep calming breath, he asks in a controlled soft voice, barely above a whisper, "You are just now telling me that those two crazy fairies live in this forest! You didn't think to tell me this before?"

Asher, suddenly feeling very uncomfortable, just shrugs and says, "You never asked."

Daghan, trying really hard to keep his patience, asks Asher, "Is there anything else you might want to tell me at this point? Do Kieran's assassins live close by, ogres, dragons, or giant rock people perhaps? Anything or anyone that you can think of, because I'm asking now!"

Asher remains silent for a moment and then simply replies, "Well, let's see, we got giant fire spittin' toads!"

"Yep! That be true," Finn adds. "And then there is the fact that this forest has a lot of plants and dead things that will try to suck the life out of us, oh and imps. Ornery little imps. Snarky little things, really. They mess with your head, they do," he says, tapping a finger on the side of his head. "Other than all of them, no."

Daghan looks at the three brothers and then at the woman sitting behind Asher. The human woman has remained quiet during all that has transpired with the elves. She now looks from Daghan to where Sadie is still sleeping peacefully and asks, "Is my granddaughter all right?"

Daghan looks at Finn with a stink-eye of his own and snaps, "Wake her!"

Finn shrugs, and as he does so Sadie picks her head up off of his shoulder and yawns, stretching her arms above her head she looks around and then asks, "What's going on? I must have dozed off." Blinking a few times and then rubbing her eyes, she looks around some more, smiles happily, and asks, "Did I miss anything?"

# A PAINFUL REMINDER

Arguing as usual over which potions to take and which spells will use the least of their limited magic, it catches them off guard when a force of great power suddenly takes hold of them. It feels as if a giant hand has reached out of nowhere and wrapped itself around each of them, keeping them suspended, demanding all of their attention, and in their minds they hear the familiar voice of their king.

"What are the two of you doing?"

"Master!" Ezra says. "There is a band of strangers traveling through these woods. We are following them to test a new potion on them for you, my lord."

"The ones the two of you are following are not just common travelers, you fools! The queen's granddaughter, *my heir*, is alive! The treacherous witch lied to me! I have sealed all the portals and posted guards at them. The girl travels with Daghan, three elves from her mothers' troop and a human female. You must not underestimate Daghan or the queen herself! Do you understand? I do not want the child to escape!" he thunders.

"Yes, master!" They reply as they hang in the air, unable to move.

"I need the two of you at the top of the mountain where you will have a good view of anyone or anything trying to get to the top. There is a reason why they are climbing this mountain, and I want to know what it is! Gather all your potions and transport to the top, and do not fail me! I will contact you later."

"Yes, master." Eagerly they agree but then start to complain. "My king," Ezra whines. "We do not have enough powers to do all that you have asked of us."

As his frustration and impatience grows so does the pressure with which he holds them. Their bodies are squeezed as his magic tightens around them. Alarmed, they try to squirm free only to feel the pressure grow even tighter. "What did you say? I'm sure I must have misunderstood you!" he says sarcastically, an unseen smile on his handsome face.

They are unable to draw a single breath and feel as if their bones are going to start snapping from the pressure, and his magic tightens just a little more.

*Pain, hideous pain!* Their bodies are wracked with it, their screams echoing through their minds.

Suddenly they're released, they drop to the ground landing flat on their backs and they slowly try to suck in air. Rolling onto their sides, they struggle to their knees, and hunched over they rock back and forth as they wait for the pain to ease. Just as suddenly as he appeared, he is gone from their minds. The memory of their king enjoying their pain lingers for a while after he is gone. It's a reminder not to whine or question him, ever! When they are finally ready, they hold hands once again to combine their powers and disappear.

At the top of the mountain not far from the falls they find a small ledge. Secluded by bushes on both sides, Ezra takes the potions and other supplies and begins arranging them in order. Zara goes in search of the fresh ingredients they will need to complete their potion. When she returns having found and caught what they needed, Ezra begin the task of measuring and mixing everything together.

Ezra looks at the final ingredient Zara hands her and smiles. "This is a very nice batch of yellow spotted toadstool worms you found, very nice."

Zara, blushing slightly from the high praise, says, "Yes, I felt very fortunate to have happened upon them. I knew you would be pleased. Those little beauties will work nicely to change the young princess for our king."

Caught up in their individual tasks, neither notices the stranger approaching from behind until he is right behind them looking over their shoulders. They each get a slight prickling sensation starting at the nape of their necks that travels down their spine. They look at each other and glance over their shoulders. They jump, startled to find a stranger looming over them.

"What is that horrible smell?" he asks as he covers his nose.

Looking up at the intruder, they assume that he is one of the king's assassins because of the scar on his face.

Not recognizing him by sight, Ezra says, "State your business and who you are!"

The assassin smiles, having no intention of telling them his business or his name. Only the king knows the names of his assassins. To know a fairy's true name gives you the ability to control them, no matter how powerful they are. This is why fairies never give their full name.

Studying him, they think he is handsome even though he has a wicked, sickle-shaped scar that runs from nose to cheek under his left eye. He grins at them again, and it is not a grin of mirth but one of evil intent. "The king is coming with a small army, though I do not see why he will need such a force to take down this small band of travelers."

Ezra looks at him and says, "Do not underestimate these travelers. The king has told us that it is the granddaughter to the queen herself that travels with an escort. A human woman, three elves from the princess's troop, and Daghan, the queen's mightiest warrior."

The assassin shows no sign of the inner turmoil that this news causes him. One minute he is standing behind them, and the next he is gone without a sound.

Looking at Zara, Ezra says, "Assassins make my skin crawl with all their sneaking around."

Zara, nodding her head in agreement, goes back to work trimming and measuring the ingredients for Ezra. Finally finishing the last potion they gather everything together and prepare for the coming storm, neither of them looking forward to the battle that looms ahead.


The wind around them begins to pick up, blowing harder, pulling at their clothes and whipping their hair into their faces. Daghan, finally back to his normal self, reaches out with his magic and searches the upper portion of the mountain looking for a cave or some other sort of protection they can seek shelter in.

"I did not find much in the way of protection," he informs the others.

Everyone in the troop agrees that it would be best to keep climbing, and Finn puts Sadie in front of him as Baba scoots closer to Asher's back.

"I'm thinkin' the storm is goin' to get much worse than this!" Asher says as he looks around, glancing toward the top of the mountain. "Much worse."

"I'm feelin' the same, but there's nothin' we can do about it now," Finn says, noticing that Asher seems to be preoccupied with looking for something. Finn glances at Bohdi on his shoulder, and they both decide it would be best to stay sharp.

Daghan looks around for Bohdi and finds him sitting on the back of his owl, perched on Finn's shoulder. "Everyone's accounted for; let's move out!"

Swinging through the trees, which is how he normally likes to travel, Daghan is constantly having to dodge their branches to keep from being thrashed by them as the trees are whipped back and forth in the wind. Knowing that he won't be able to keep up with the others on foot, he decides to call for his own pet. He doesn't usually call on her in the presence of others, because they have a tendency to run away screaming.

"I can't travel through the trees any longer. The wind is too strong! I'm going to call for my pet. Don't be alarmed when you see her. She won't harm you; I promise."

Seconds later a huge black spider walks onto the ledge just above their heads. She suddenly jumps down, landing in front of Daghan and startling the rest of the troop.

"What? Her name is Arabella. She's a giant black widow. Beautiful, isn't she? Hmm, hmm?" he says, wiggling his eyebrows up and down, fully expecting that revelation to put them at ease.

The spider stands eight feet in height, so it's easy for all to see the red hourglass on the underside of her abdomen. Her shiny black exoskeleton gleams in the moonlight. The bottom sections of all her legs are covered in coarse black hairs that seem to be more like spikes than actual hair. All eight of her eyes give off a greenish glow that just adds to her overall creepiness.

Swinging up onto her back, Daghan looks around at the group and asks, "What? She's perfectly safe!"

Daghan notices Asher and Finn stroking the necks of their pets, murmuring to them in quiet tones of reassurance. The bear and wolverine watch the giant spider suspiciously.

Hoping to put everyone more at ease Daghan and Arabella take the lead.

Asher, wanting to speak privately with Daghan, nudges Arlo to catch up with him. Coming up alongside them but keeping a respectful distance, he strikes up a conversation. "I'd like to speak with you for a moment, if ya doona mind?"

Daghan, cocking one eyebrow up in question, looks over at him and waits for him to continue.

Asher begins speaking in elven so the female riding with him won't understand what he is saying. "I've been thinking—I feel the need to tell you that I have a certain ability not common in elves. An ability that I think just might come in handy if things start to turn bad on this journey."

Daghan studies him quietly and then decides to keep his attitude aloof for the moment. Continuing to speak in elven he replies, "An ability, you say. What kind of ability are you referring to?"

Not knowing if Daghan will become angry, Asher sheepishly glances at him and then blurts out, "I have the ability to make myself invisible and then transport to another location while remaining invisible. Oh, and Arlo can do so as well."

Daghan doesn't quite know how to respond to this revelation. He decides to ask a question: "Can you transport others like that or just yourself?"

Asher thinks for a moment and then replies, "I doona really know. I have never tried to make someone else invisible and transport them with me."

Daghan looks at Asher for a long moment and then says, "Well, it might be a good idea for you to find out if you can. You know, before something happens. It's just a suggestion."

During their conversation, the wind picks up considerably. Swirling around them, it blows dirt and debris up into their faces. Covering their eyes, they try to hide them from the stinging debris as they look straight up. Enormous dark clouds quickly move in overhead, forming a supercell as they watch. A bolt of lightning flashes, illuminating the entire thunderhead. Released, it races toward the ground, striking very close to them, causing the hair on their bodies to stand on end. The clap of thunder that follows is so loud that it hurts their ears. Torrential rain begins to pour down on them. The storm is upon them and they are out of time; they must find some sort of shelter.

# I SPY WITH MY FAIRY EYE

Just a few feet away, three small forms emerge from their cave. Tricky little creatures that usually only come out at night to forage for food and other stuff they need, have come out to investigate the storm.. The pouring rain doesn't bother them; in fact they seem to like it. The biggest one hears something close by, and quietly creeping through the night what they find intrigues them: a small troop of travelers loitering much too close to the entrance to their home. They hunker down in some bushes and silently begin washing the dust from their bodies with the rain, all the while keeping a close eye on the travelers. They are very good at being very quiet; where they live their lives depend on it sometimes.

Lightning streaks through the sky again and again, striking the ground and then a tree not too far from Sadie. The claps of thunder are loud and sharp. She ducks and covers her ears, and leaning back into Finn she starts whimpering. Finn tries to comfort her without success. Baba, knowing Sadie doesn't like loud storms, asks Asher to turn back, but instead he whistles for Finn to catch up. Ryder sprints the few yards it takes to get to them.

Baba reaches out to Sadie and takes her from Finn. Seating her between Asher and herself, she drops her head to Sadie's ear, whispering, "There, all snug and safe. Everything will be fine; you'll see."

A bolt of lightning slams into the ground just a few feet from them. The shock wave knocks Baba and Sadie off Arlo's back as the bear bolts up the side of the mountain. They hit the ground hard, flat on their backs, knocking the wind out of both of them.

Sadie is momentarily stunned, lying on the ground on her back, unable to breathe or cry. The knot in her chest spreads to her stomach, making it even harder for her to draw a breath. As she tries to relax, the knot tightens, and pain pulses through her body as a couple of tears slip from her eyes. Lying on her back struggling to breathe, she feels the hair on the nape of her neck begin to tingle. Looking around her, she catches sight of something out of the corner of her eye. Turning onto her side, her eyes widen in surprise, because just a few feet away she sees four pair of glowing eyes. Three sets glow red and blink in and out from behind the bushes directly in front of her. One set, farther back, stares straight at her, unblinking, the glowing yellow orbs fierce, hungry. Frightened, she grabs ahold of Baba's shirt and starts yanking on it with one hand as she unconsciously scratches her head with the other.

Finally able to suck in small amounts of air she rolls onto her back again. Staring straight up, the glowing eyes forgotten for the moment, she sips at the air. "Saadieee ..." the haunting voice quietly calls to her.

As Baba turns to face Sadie she sees her staring straight up, a terrified look on her face. That's when she also notices the glowing eyes, and panic grips her as she croaks, "Daghan! Daghan!" That's all she can manage to say.

As the three are quietly enjoying a nice wash in the rain behind some bushes they suddenly stop, their big eyes bulging as a giant spider quickly darts into view. Not knowing what to do they turn and run, heading straight for the opening to their cave. Ducking inside, breathing hard, they wait and listen. It doesn't take long before they hear the rustling as something quickly makes its way closer to where they are hiding.

Slasher, the biggest one of the bunch, chances a look outside. At first he doesn't see anything because of the heavy driving rain, and then he notices the spiky legs, all eight of them.

Looking down, Daghan can see an opening. It looks to be a small cave, and just inside he can see three pairs of red glowing eye bobbing around and blinking in and out. Leaning sideways, he tries to get a better look inside, a steady stream of water running across his face. "We do not mean to harm you. We just need a place to wait out the storm," he says, wiping the water from his eyes and nose as another bolt of lightning streaks through the treetops directly above him. He unconsciously ducks his head as he says, "May we come inside to get out of the storm?"

After much pushing and shoving Slasher steps away from his two companions, Slade and Scallywag, who both gently push at him. Slapping their hands away, he steps out of the cave opening. Looking up at Daghan, he says, "And why should we be helping the likes of you?"

"A *gollywoggle*?" Daghan is surprised to see one, because he has not seen a gollywoggle in many years.

Small in size, usually no taller than three, maybe three and a half feet, they have round balding heads with a small patch of scruffy hair on top that hangs down between long pointy, floppy ears. They have little potbellies and skinny arms and legs with surprisingly big hands and feet. They come from a realm called Tortuga, where their kind has adapted the human pirate culture. They talk, dress, and act like pirates.

Remembering how curious the little creatures are, he says, "I've got a human traveling with us." Looking down at him, he wiggles his eyebrows up and down. "Hmm? A human! A female human!"

Knowing that's all it will take, Daghan calls for the rest of the troop to follow him. Arabella disappears, leaving Daghan standing in front of the cave, and the others follow suit as one by one their pets disappear. As Asher and Finn help Sadie and Baba, Daghan ducks his head and steps inside. The cave is dark but dry, and another bolt of lightning strikes the ground just outside. Glad to be out of the storm, they huddle together for warmth just inside the small cave.

# A CAVERNOUS MISTAKE

Feeling better now that she can breathe, Sadie tries to look around. Looking above her head and to either side all she can see is rock. Sandwiched between Baba and Finn, she can't see anything in front or behind her, and she begins to feel as if the walls of the tunnel are closing in on her. Holding onto Baba's belt loop, she shuffles forward. The air around her seems hotter, stuffier. Tilting her head back, she looks up, trying to find some cooler air, all the while thinking to herself, *It should be much darker in here.*

The narrow passage ends abruptly and opens into a wide, deep cavern. Stalactites in many different sizes hang from the ceiling loaded with glowing crystals of all shapes and sizes. The ceiling itself has clusters of glowing crystals like stars in the night sky. The floor of the cavern has just a few short, blunt stalagmites scattered here and there like tables arranged haphazardly in a very large room. In the quiet of the cavern they can hear the rumbling thunder of a waterfall.

Daghan can see that there are several tunnel openings around the outer edges of the cavern. "Where do those lead?" he asks Slasher.

"Nowhere that concerns the likes of you!" he snarks. Pushing the two smaller gollywoggles in front of him, he motions for the rest of them to follow. Snickering amongst themselves, they keep looking back at Sadie and Baba.

They lead them down an old stairway carved into the bedrock. Gently sloping downward, it then levels out and disappears as they reach the bottom of the cave.

Sadie's eyes widen as she takes in the scene before her, and she remarks, "This cave is enormous!" her voice echoing through the cavern. "It looks even bigger from down here on the ground." She notices a dusty smell mixed with a stinky odor she doesn't recognize. "Ewe, that stinks!" Wrinkling her nose in distaste, she pulls her shirt up over it and continues on with the others.

Daghan, looking around, can't help but feel that somehow this cave is familiar to him, even though he knows for certain he's never been there before.

Walking across the wide expanse of the cavern floor, Sadie again holds on tight to Baba's belt loop as she looks around. She gives it a tug to get her attention. "Baba, do you see how those gollywoggles keep looking at us? You don't think they eat people do you?"

Baba laughs and says, "I don't think Daghan would have brought us in here if they were going to eat us, do you?"

"Baba, I saw their teeth! Didn't you see their teeth? They have very sharp-looking teeth!"

Chuckling, she hugs Sadie to her side. "Don't worry, I won't let anything eat you; I promise!"

"They talk like *pirates*, Baba, *pirates*! Don't you think that's weird?"

"Yes but in a funny sort of way. Don't worry!"

Sadie, still not convinced, decides to keep a close watchful eye on the gollywoggles. "They're up to no good. I just know it!" she mumbles to herself.

Gliding through the air on his pet, a monstrous flying lizard he calls Gothock, the king of darkness makes his way to the Nocturnal Forest where his minions await his arrival. It would be much quicker for him to transport there, but he prefers to travel with his pet, enjoying the feel of the air as it rushes past him, his beautiful long black hair flying loose in the wind. He also enjoys the fear he sees in everyone's eyes as they get a good look at Gothock. "You really are quite the gruesome sight, ol' boy," he says, reaching down and patting his neck.

The gigantic winged lizard preens under his master's praises, being all brawn and no brains. He is still an excellent hunter. A steady stream of poisonous saliva drips from his jaws, forming long slimy strands. His forked tongue flicks in and out, tasting the air as he flies, his beady black eyes watchful. Patience is Gothock's virtue. He is always calmly waiting for that one opportunity, that one moment in time when his victim's guard is down, that one fraction of an instant that it takes to strike. One small bite and then patience on his part as the poison slowly works its way through the body. His victim becomes disoriented while trying desperately to get away, but they never get away. All he has to do is follow their scent at his own leisurely, lumbering pace, his tongue flicking in and out so he can taste their fear as he tracks them down.

Suddenly Kieran's face loses all signs of joy and he concentrates, but the connection he had with Yamanu, the wraith-like creature McWeenie created for him to follow Sadie is gone. Bellowing in rage his scream breaks the silence of the night. Dramatically he reaches toward the sky, his fingers curling like claws, and yells, "Why me? Why me?" Dejectedly he hangs his head in misery as Gothock flies on.


Sitting on their ledge, Ezra and Zara wait for another bolt to strike. Their wait isn't long, because the storm they created has formed into a huge supercell. They laugh and hoot as the lightning repeatedly strikes the surrounding area. The storm is now at its full strength, producing hail, torrential rains, and hammering winds. Another bolt illuminates the massive thunderhead as a loud *boom* rolls across the sky immediately followed by a loud *crack* as the lightning is released, streaking downward to strike a tree, causing it to explode.

"Wow! That was a good one!" Zara says.

Ezra, almost giddy with delight, turns to Zara and comments, "This is an excellent spot to watch the show. I really do love storms." Rubbing her hands together excitedly, she claps as another enormous bolt streaks through the sky. This one splits into smaller pieces of itself all racing in different directions. Some of them flash through the clouds. One arm of it speeds toward the ground, slamming into it with such force it shakes the mountain.

Laughing and hooting, they clap their hands and raise them high above their heads as they call out to the heavens. "More power! More power!" they yell.

On the ground below them, the assassin is crouched behind a fallen boulder, not much in the way of cover but better than standing in the open. He looks up and pitches the two old crones an evil look. Soaked to his bones by the heavy downpour of rain, the wind lashing it against him, the rain stings his face and hands like a thousand tiny whips. "I'll take care of the two of you later!" he snarks as he stalks off in search of his prey. Smiling wickedly, he thinks of all the delicious ways he can make them scream and beg for mercy. Just the thought of making those two suffer puts him in a better mood.

Inside the cavern, Sadie gazes up at the twinkling lights; she's in awe of its beauty. The stalactites cling to the roof of the immense cave like sharp sparkling teeth, the crystals giving off a soft hazy glow. *Beautiful, but kind of creepy too*, she thinks. In the deep dark recesses of the cavern's ceiling, where the smaller crystals barely give off any light, Sadie thinks she can see something moving around. The smaller lights blink in and out, giving the effect of something crawling across the top of the cavern and around the bases of some of the stalactites.

*Creepy*, she thinks again as she resumes walking beside Baba. Looking back up over her shoulder, she is sure she sees something moving up there. "It's probably just a bat. That's it, a *really big bat*." She decides not to worry about it for now, but she can't help glancing up there every now and then.

Daghan and the three elves keep an eye out for any kind of movement toward the far end of the cave. "There's something that seems off about this cave. I'm just not sure what it is," Daghan says, remaining relaxed but ready. "I knows this cave; it's familiar somehow."

"So you have been in here before?" Bohdi asks.

Thinking, Daghan searches his mind. Looking over at the elves he can tell that they seem uneasy too. Frustrated he says, "No." He is unable to recall why this cave should seem so familiar to him. He focuses his attention on some liquid that has pooled below the stalactite directly in front of him. Looking around he notices several of the small pools around the cavern. He watches the liquid drip from the tip of the stalactite for a moment and looks at the three elves standing next to him. "I wonder if that might be the cause of the unpleasant odor that wafts through the cavern."

As he walks toward the small pool, a strong stench assaults him. His nose and eyes start to sting, and rearing back he calls over his shoulder, "This is definitely what's causing the noxious odor!" Covering his nose and squinting his eyes, he looks down into the small pool. The viscous material looks just like clear water, but the toxic smell and his stinging eyes and nose assure him that it's not. Using the toe of his boot he pushes a rock into the pool of liquid, where it quickly starts to dissolve. *Acid, and a very potent one at that.* Thinking that the acid might come in handy at some point he forms a pouch with his webbing and with a whisper reinforces it. Carefully placing the pouch under the tip of the stalactite, he fills it and then seals it, and looking around he tucks it away.

Walking back toward the elves, it hits him—*the Cave of Dark Dreams!* Daghan looks around and whispers, "Where all the horrible things from young fairies nightmares are trapped."

"Hey!" he calls. "I know where we are! We're in the Cave of Dark Dreams!"

The three elves scoot closer together as their eyes scan the cave. "No, it canna be!" Asher says with a note of wonder in his voice.

While growing up, young fairies sometimes have nightmares, and their nightmares release dark magic. When released, the dark magic can and often does turn into the very things that make their dreams a nightmare.

Some time ago the queen cast a spell to trap all that dark magic. She released her spell into the web that connects all fae in Otherworld. Once the dark magic is collected it's buried deep inside a mountain. The dark magic is bound to the mountain, trapped inside, never allowed to leave.

All fairy children are told the story of the Cave of Dark Dreams so they won't be afraid of their nightmares coming true.

"This is why the mountain comes to life at night," Asher whispers.

"And why the dead rise up and try to suck the life out-o-us!" Finn whispers while massaging his neck. "Our grandda once told me that the cave is one of great beauty, where the dark magic breathes life back into the dead, causing them to rise up and walk the night. *Hungry*, he said they are*! Always hungry*!" Finn gulps.

"Their ancient eyes glow in the darkness, their inner sight always searching. They are creatures with a deep gnawing hunger. It is said that if a fairy is ever bitten by one of the dead, it drains their magic, their life force to revive itself, leaving the fairy an empty, ghoulish wraith that wanders the forest in search of warmth." Even Daghan, the queen's mightiest warrior, shivers as he remembers the tales from his youth.

Boom, boom, boom, boom! There is the sound of several consecutive dull thuds, and then the ground beneath everyone's feet begins to shake and roll, throwing everyone off balance and knocking some to the ground. As if something under the mountain is trying to stand, it groans, trembles, and shakes from the force of what Daghan thinks is lightning striking the ground outside. The whole cavern continues to shake violently, and rocks and dirt tumble down the walls onto the floor. The stalactites begin to shake, and cracks form around the base of some. Others form cracks that run the length of their long pointy columns, their crystals popping out and falling to the cavern floor where they shatter into tiny pieces. Larger chunks of debris begin to rain down from above.

Everyone is looking for someplace to hide. Trying to stay on their feet as the floor of the cavern rolls and shakes, they head for the tunnel openings, stumbling and falling as they go and having to stop and start as they dodge the falling debris.

Scrambling to get out of the way of falling debris and looking for a safe place to hide, no one notices that the cavern's ceiling has come alive with activity. The creatures have become bolder, slinking out of the deep shadows to quickly crawl across the ceiling and align themselves with the top of the walls. They cling to the walls above the openings, waiting for a chance to snatch one of the troop and drag them away. "Hungry, so hungry!"

The noise inside the cavern has become thunderous, making it hard to communicate with one another. Daghan yells at the top of his voice, "Everyone! Stay away from the pools of liquid!"

Sadie, holding on as tight as she can to Baba's hand, is unable to run as fast as everyone else. Baba, pulling her along, doesn't see the massive stalactite above them break free from the roof of the cavern.

Asher looks over just in time to see it break loose with Sadie and Baba directly underneath it. With a thought he transports himself to their location, moving so fast he creates a blast of air in his wake. He snatches them from under the massive structure a split second before it crashes to the ground. Reappearing near a tunnel entrance, Sadie and Baba are huddled in Asher's embrace, their backs pressed to the wall of the cave, his body protecting them. They just stare at him for a long moment as Asher gulps in air, huffing and puffing from the exertion of moving at such a high speed and carrying two other people, their faces blank from the shock of being whisked away at such a high speed. Turning around, they all see the spot where they had just been standing, the huge stalactite now a mountain of rubble with a cloud of dust surrounding it. Its crystals are strewn across the cavern floor. Still bug-eyed, they look at Asher. He smiles, feeling quite pleased with himself.

Daghan walks up to them and slaps Asher on the back, saying, "Well, that answers that question, doesn't it?"

Baba places her hand on the side of Asher's face. Caressing it, she smiles and says, "We owe you our lives."

Sadie wraps her arms around his waist and gives him a fierce hug. Looking up at him, she says, "That was so cool. Can we do it again sometime, just for fun?"

Asher, feeling drained from the exertion of moving that fast, just shakes his head as he blows out a long slow breath.

The troop gathers together to view the damage done to the cavern. The shaking has stopped for now, and everyone is talking all at once except for Sadie; she's keeping a close eye on the gollywoggles, who are standing a few feet away by another tunnel opening. She watches them as their eyes survey the ceiling of the cavern. She doesn't like the expressions on their faces, and following their line of sight her eyes probe the dark recesses of the ceiling as well. *They know what's up there, and they're afraid of whatever it is!*

Looking across the cavern, Sadie gets that tingly feeling at the nape of her neck again, and her eyes are drawn to the stairway where they entered the cave. Squinting because of the low light and all the dust in the air, she can barely make out a pair of glowing yellow eyes in the midst of a large shadow. Yanking on Asher's shirt to get his attention, she points in the direction of the eyes. "Look, do you see the eyes?"

Asher looks and sees nothing and asks, "What eyes?"

"There!" Sadie points. "By the stairway that we walked down."

Asher, using a bit of magic to light the stairway, replies, "I doona see anything."

Sadie, frowning and sounding a bit put out, says, "Never mind; they're gone!"

Daghan looks around, doing a head count. The gollywoggles are standing by another tunnel entrance a few feet away. He watches them as they scan the ceiling of the cavern, but glancing upward, he doesn't notice anything out of the ordinary. His eyes travel back to his troop, making sure everyone is there. He sees Sadie watching the gollywoggles as well. Then she turns toward the opening where they entered the cavern. He watches as she tugs on Asher's shirt. He can't hear what she is saying, but he can tell that she is upset about something. As she points to the stairway he follows her line of sight and catches a glimpse of glowing yellow eyes, and then they are gone. Not liking the feeling he got from those eyes, he decides to make sure Sadie stays close to Asher or himself because whatever that was he is positive that she is right—something is following her.

Entering a tunnel, the gollywoggles leading the way, Daghan puts Sadie in between himself and Asher, telling Asher, "Stay alert! And don't let Sadie out of your sight!"

Asher looks around as they enter the tunnel and wonders how long he will be able to keep her in his sight as the darkness swallows them.

Baba falls into step behind Asher with Bohdi and Finn behind her. They stay in single file even though this tunnel is quite a bit wider than the last one. Soon the soft glow of the cavern is gone, and some of the troop find themselves surrounded by a complete and total darkness. Baba, unable to see anything at all, keeps a portion of Asher's shirt gripped in a tight fist of one hand while the other hand is placed firmly in the middle of his back.

The elves growing a little uneasy, having always been accustomed to being able to see just fine in the darkness of night due to the fact that there is always some small source of light, the moon or the stars. But this darkness is absolute; no light source reaches these tunnels.

Sadie doesn't realize how dark the tunnel is, because even though she can't see perfectly she is able to see everyone's shape and the outline of their faces well enough to know whom she is looking at.

Daghan feels completely at home in the absolute darkness of the tunnels. He is fully adapted to the absence of light. His night vision allows him to see shapes well enough, and his arachnid senses allow him to feel his way through the darkness. But even he doesn't see or feel what slips inside the tunnel with them.

Asher, unable to see Sadie, now whispers into the blackness, "My inner light," and a small flame appears, floating in the air just above and to the right of his head. The small flame bathes the troop in a soft yellow glow. Relieved, Baba blinks and loosens her grip on Asher's shirt.

The creature that's been following them stops, ducking back into the darkness. Clinging to the ceiling it waits until the light grows dim as the troop travels further down the tunnel. *Hungry, so hungry!*

The endless walking through the labyrinth of passageways gives Sadie a chance to think about everything that's been happening to her. She tries to find her power to produce a flame of her own; she just can't figure out where the power comes from. While concentrating, Sadie realizes that she can hear the gollywoggles whispering to each other up ahead, but she can't understand what they are saying. Peering around Daghan, she watches them arguing about something, slapping and poking each other, the biggest one pushing the other two in the direction he wants them to go. Every once in a while they take turns looking back at the troop.

Suddenly Sadie doesn't like being in the tunnel anymore; there's not enough air to breathe. Stepping out of line to her right she feels a little better, no longer being sandwiched between Daghan and Asher. The tunnel takes a sharp left and then a sharp right and ends abruptly, opening into a larger area with three tunnels all leading off in a different direction. Sadie, still standing out of line to the right, is peeking down the nearest tunnel. She can see glowing crystals winking in and out farther down.

Daghan, watching the gollywoggles argue, finally says, "Well, which one takes us to the falls?"

Slasher points and says, "The correct tunnel be that one on yer far left." He starts walking in that direction, Slade and Scallywag following him.

Daghan and the rest of the troop follow the gollywoggles, Sadie, still looking down the tunnel, doesn't notice the others walk away. Asher stops suddenly and looks around for Sadie. He sees her peering down the other tunnel several feet away, and just when he is about to say, "Sadie come on," the words die in his throat. He watches in horror as a long, thin tail slowly drops down from the ceiling.

Asher yells, "Sadie duck down!" But it's too late—the tail wraps around her midsection and Sadie is lifted off the floor, kicking and thrashing with all her might. She looks at Asher and starts screaming. In a flash she's gone, disappearing into the same tunnel that she had been looking in, her screams echoing as they grow more distant.

Horrified, Asher takes off, running and ducking into the tunnel. The rest of the troop takes off after Asher, but by the time they all reach the tunnel entrance all they see is a faint glow disappear around a corner. They soon find that this tunnel breaks off into several other tunnels every few feet.

Ducking his head in tunnel after tunnel, Asher listens for the faint sound of Sadie screaming. Desperate and realizing that the creature has outdistanced him, Asher runs as fast as he can, taking first one tunnel and then another, his flame keeping pace with him. Rounding a corner he comes to another Y in the tunnel. Listening, he can't hear her screaming anymore. Panicked and out of breath, his heart pounding like a sledgehammer in his chest, he beats his fist against the wall as he yells, "Sadie! Sadie!" Listening, all he hears now is his own voice echoing through the tunnels.

After a few seconds, nothing but the sound of his own heavy breathing breaks the silence. The rest of the troop finally catches up to him, Finn and Bohdi with flames of their own. They watch helplessly as he ducks his head into each tunnel, listening for any noise.

Daghan walks up behind him and lays a hand on his shoulder. "I've lost the wee lass, Daghan! You put me in charge of her and I've lost her. I couldna even keep her safe for a wee while."

"It's not your fault. We all let her down. The only thing we can do now is find her, and we will." Daghan steps around him. "Let me try. I'm used to finding my way in this kind of darkness." He places his hands on the walls of the first tunnel. Concentrating, he reaches out with his magic, looking for Sadie's essence; hands flat against the walls he waits. Feeling for the faintest vibrations in the walls, he moves from one tunnel to the next feeling his way along the walls. Finally he picks up on the barest whisper of movement.

"This way. Be as quiet as possible," he whispers.

Much slower than before, they make their way through the mountain's labyrinth, Daghan allowing the walls to tell him which way they need to go, all the while wishing Sadie would make some kind of noise.

Baba, fear for Sadie humming through her body, keeps her hand over her mouth to hold back the sobs threatening to escape as she silently prays for her safety. They all walk silently as they all move slowly forward as one. Daghan, his head down in concentration, switches tunnels once again, and his head snaps up as a scream pierces the quiet. Everyone listens to the echoes as they slowly roll away. Just one scream and then nothing but cloying silence. Hope surges to life in Daghan, because that scream was closer and it means that Sadie is still alive.

They all race down the tunnel the scream came from, Asher pushing the others out of his way. He catches Daghan just as they both burst through the opening of another cave. Skidding to a halt behind Daghan, Asher braces for the impact that is sure to follow as each person behind him runs into the back of the person in front of them. The sight that greets all of them is terrifying.


The gollywoggles, knowing most of the tunnels and caves like the backs of their hands, are in no hurry to catch up. They know what took the little girl, and the thought of what is going to happen to her makes them shiver. After all, the three of them were only wanting to have a little fun at the stranger's expense.

"Poor little girl," Slade says, lowering his head.

"The loss of one so young is a sad thing to be sure," Scallywag intones.

Slasher looks at his companions, saying, "Aye, tis a sad, sad thing. Do you know what will be making us even sadder? *Daghan!* That's what!" He yells in their faces as he slaps the both of them upside the backs of their heads. "Daghan will be making *us* vera sad when he gets ahold of us! Let me think, think, Slasher! We need to split up. Aye, we split up and find them. We find them, and then we help them get to the falls just like we said we would."

"That be a right good plan, Slasher. Do ye know where we be now? Because I be thinkin' we're lost," Slade says.

"I be lost too, Slasher," Scallywag says, backing Slade.

Being lost too but not wanting to admit to it, Slasher says, "Fine! I'll take this tunnel." He points to the one right in front of him. "Scallywag, ye take that one," he says, pointing to his right. "And Slade ye can take that one," he says, pointing to his left. "When we find the others, we each stay out of sight till we all be together again, aye?"

Slade and Scallywag bob their heads in agreement. Slasher pushes each in the direction of their tunnels.

# YAMANU

In the center of the cave is an immense timber wolf lying on the floor casually feeding on the carcass of what they all assume is what's left of the creature that took Sadie, its body torn apart, pieces of it littering the floor around the massive wolf.

Asher hears a faint noise off to his left. It's Sadie, crouched down behind a large rock, quietly crying. The whole troop moves as one, shuffling very slowly toward Sadie. Baba softly calls to her. "Sadie, honey, it's Baba. Look at me, sweetheart."

Sadie lifts her head, her eyes growing wide with relief. Baba makes hand gestures, waving her over to them. Sadie scrambles on her hands and knees across the floor and into Baba's arms. "There now. You're okay, and everything is going to be fine."

The wolf doesn't seem to care; it continues to chew on the bone.

Asher moves in closer to Sadie and Baba. The need he has to hold Sadie is like a living thing that won't be denied. Taking her from Baba, he hugs her tightly and breathes in her child scent. Then they all slowly start to back out of the cave. The wolf lifts its massive head and turns to look at the troop. They all freeze, holding their breath, its yellow eyes probing as it roams from one to another before coming to rest on Asher.

Sadie stiffens, and Asher rubs her back as he murmurs to her softly, "Doona fret wee one; all is well."

Daghan comes up beside Asher and Sadie, putting himself between them and the wolf. Looking into those yellow eyes, he senses intelligence and a fierce protectiveness toward Sadie but no malice. He knows that this wolf is what has been tracking Sadie; he just doesn't know why. Turning, he whispers, "Back out slowly, very slowly."

As they're backing out Daghan watches the wolf stand, its lips pull back in a snarl, exposing long sharp teeth as it starts to growl, a deep rumbling growl. They all stop. No one even so much as twitches a finger. Its yellow eyes roam from one to the next. Suddenly it makes a small lung at them, its body stiff with tension. Sadie and Baba scream. It snaps at them, making a half-bark, half-growling sound as saliva sprays from its mouth, dripping onto the floor.

Daghan crouches down, holding his hands out in front of him and saying, "Easy boy, easy! We aren't going to harm her. We're just trying to help her get home." He motions for the rest of them to keep moving back into the tunnel. He watches the wolf with hooded eyes, trying his best not to challenge it by making direct eye contact. It watches the others slowly back out of the cave, and Daghan continues to speak to it softly, "We mean her no harm; besides we're the good guys. Just let us help her. That's it, stay where you are."

Once outside the cave they each breathe a sigh of relief as they head back down the tunnel, staying close together. Daghan is the last to leave, and he watches the wolf relax a little. It licks its chops before turning to mist and disappearing.

Pushing to the head of the group, Daghan sees the gollywoggles standing farther down the tunnel. He walks up to Slasher and grabs hold of him and lifts him into the air as he begins shaking him violently and yelling, "You get us out of these tunnels and topside *right now* or I will personally make a stew out of the three of you! Do you understand?"

Slasher hangs limply in Daghan's grasp, his head flopping back and forth like a rag doll from the force of being shaken repeatedly and says, "Aye, topside. I'll take ye right now!"

Landing in a clearing, Kieran dismounts, but instead of Gothock disappearing he sends him off into the forest to look for Sadie. His minions give Gothock a wide berth. Kieran reaches out with his mind, searching for her, and again he is unable to find her. He searches for Yamanu and is unable to find him either. "That no good mangy mutt! I knew I couldn't trust him!" Fuming, he throws his head back, and curling his hands into claws he reaches up into the air and releases lightning into the sky, roaring in anger as he does so. The lightning is absorbed by the storm and then thrown back at the ground, and the mountain shudders from the force of it.

Ezra and Zara, still sitting on their ledge, look at one another and say, "Our king is finally here!" They get up and gather their supplies and reach out to him, calling, "All is ready, master."

Instantly he appears behind them on the ledge, saying, "I knew that the two of you would manage without more power."

Startled, they jump and turn around.

"The two of you wouldn't happen to know where Sadie is, would you?"

Swallowing the fear that grips them, they begin to babble at the same time, "Well, you see, master, we ah …" Zara stammers.

"We've tried but we have not been able to aah …" Ezra stammers.

"We think they have gone underground," Zara says.

"Yes, underground," Ezra blurts.

"Enough!" he barks, holding up one hand. "Just one of you tell me."

Ezra swallows the lump in her throat and answers, "Well, we think that Daghan found his way inside the mountain. We believe they travel through it now, instead of up it."

"That would explain the loss of contact," he says to no one in particular. "So what's with the storm if they've gone underground? Hmm!"

"We aaah, we like storms," Ezra replies.

"Oh well, I guess they will have to come out sooner or later, won't they? But I'm tired of it." With a flick of his wrist the lightning, rain, and wind stop. Rubbing his hands together he says, "Well, show me! Come now, don't just stand there staring at me. What goodies have you made for me?"

Blinking, Ezra and Zara spring into action, bouncing off one another. They both grab something from the ledge, and Ezra is the first to start talking. "This, my lord, I am sure will please you." Holding up a small orb full of liquid and wiggly things she says, "This is an exploding orb that we made special for the queen's little granddaughter!"

The king looks more closely at it and asks, "What does it do? It won't hurt her, will it? Because I don't want her injured."

"No! No, my lord. These are merely yellow spotted toadstool parasites," Zara explains, coming up to stand beside Ezra. "You see, the parasites worm their way painlessly into their victim and then make their way to the brain. Once there they will slowly, over time of course, turn her mind dark. Slowly, very slowly, my lord, so that no one notices the change until she decides to show her true self. By then, my lord, it will be too late to save her—the cure will no longer work."

"There is a cure?"

"Yes, my lord, but not an easy one to obtain." Ezra snickers.

Telling her master, saying it out loud, causes Zara to suddenly be plagued by guilt. "The orb is for Lila's twin, a child I thought long dead." Shaking herself mentally she tries to shrug off the guilt that is fast building inside her but is unable to do so.

"Excellent!" he says. Plucking the orb from her hand, he illuminates it. He holds it up to his eyes, and peering into it he watches the tiny worms squiggle and wiggle as they swim through the liquid. "You're positive these things won't harm her?"

Ezra speaks up. "Yes, my lord. I mean no, my lord! I mean they will not harm her; they will only change the way she views her world."

Still examining the orb he says, "I believe you have out done yourselves with this little beauty!"

Ezra stands waiting, looking up at him with adoration in her wrinkled and sagging eyes. Zara remains adrift in her own thoughts.

Hesitantly, he reaches out and begins to pat first one and then the other on the head. *The things I must do for my loyal subjects!* He thinks as his stomach rebels. *This is absolutely revolting!* He taps just the tips of his fingers on the top of each of their greasy heads gingerly. *Ewe! I hate it when I have to touch them. They're so gross and ugly.* As he pats their heads bile rushes up the back of his throat. Swallowing, he brings one arm up to cover his mouth as he gags. Having nowhere else to wipe his hand off, he wipes it on the side of his pants.

Ezra, beaming from his praise and affection, stands gazing at him, a shy smile on her face. Zara comes out of her personal trance and just looks at him.

"Now, what else do you have for me?"

# A WAR OF POWERS

Rowan and Serena pace back and forth. Lila had been keeping them up to date on all that was happening until she suddenly lost contact with Sadie as she ventured deeper into the cave. She then burst into uncontrollable tears, crying hysterically as the separation from Sadie is physically painful for her. Princess Serena casts a spell to soothe her. Lila now lies on her side curled into a ball on the couch, quietly weeping off and on.

Serena trusts Daghan, but still. "The Cave of Dark Dreams? Who would have thought that they would find their way into it?"

"For the love of all things magic!" Rowan thunders. "I do not know how much longer I can just wait here and do nothing." Turning, he says, "That's our daughter out there. She's being hunted by Kieran himself. As if that isn't bad enough, now she's gone into the Cave of Dark Dreams! Who knows what's in there. What are we doing staying here at home, Serena? We should be with her, protecting her!"

Feeling his anger and frustration, Serena walks up to him and wraps her arms around him. She croons softly, caressing the back of his neck, "We agreed that the fewer to travel the better, remember? Besides, we could not leave Lila here alone, nor could we take her with us." Leaning back she takes his face in her hands. Looking deep into his eyes she sees and feels his desperation.

He reaches up and gently takes her hands into his and kisses each one. "I know, but what if we were wrong?" Lowering his voice he whispers, "I am her father, Serena. I am the one that is supposed to protect her. I have only just today gotten the daughter I thought dead all these years back into my life. I haven't even gotten to hold her in my arms yet. What would you have me do, hmm?"

Serena, unable to stand seeing him like this, says, "Go! Go to our daughter! But remember, Rowan, you also have Lila and me here waiting for you, so take care, my love, and come home safely."

Before Rowan leaves he sits down at the table and calls Lila to him. She uncurls on the couch and gets up, sniffling. She walks to her father and climbs onto his lap.

Wrapping his arms around her he says, "I am going to make sure that your sister is well and see that she gets home safely. So no more crying, all right? You know how it undoes me to see even a single tear shine in your beautiful eyes." Holding her tightly he breathes her in. "Now take care of your mother." He lowers his voice so only she can hear him, "She needs you right now, just as much as you need her. Do not be fooled by her show of strength. She is not as strong as she would have you believe, at least not in this particular situation, hmm." He wipes the tears from her eyes and gives her a kiss on the forehead. "Now, I will return in no time and all will be as it should."

He stands holding Lila in his arms and looking at Serena, and she walks over to them, wrapping them both in a tight embrace. Rowan disappears, leaving Serena holding Lila.

Keeping the gollywoggles close to him Daghan soon realizes that they have no idea where they are. "Why don't you just admit that you're lost, Slasher?"

"Cuz I ain't lost. I just be turned around cuz of all of you, takin' off and chasin' that thing that took the wee girl. It ain't me fault! I just gotta find me way again tis all!" he whispers over his shoulder, trudging through the darkness.

"What was that thing anyway?" Daghan asks. "Are there more of them?"

"More? Oh aye, there be more! Makes me toes curl to think on all that be slitherin' through these dark tunnels," Slade says as he looks up. "An' those won't be the worst of them neither. There be all kinds of evil, heinous beasties down here," he whispers, shivering at the thought of what he has seen in the tunnels.

"Our kind have lost a lot of kin cuz of the soulless beasties that live in this mountain," Scallywag says, jumping into the conversation. "Fate be an unkind mistress to be sure."

"What else is down here? What do you call them?" Finn asks.

"We have no names for them! They ain't the same when ye see them again. They change!" Slasher murmurs as he looks all around.

"Can we fight them—I mean with magic?" Daghan asks.

"*No!* No magic!" Slasher yells, frantically slicing his hand through the air. He stops and slaps his hands over his mouth and the turns around and looks up at the ceiling and then at the rest of the troop. Removing his hands from his mouth he whispers, "They be wantin' our life force, our magic!" Stepping closer to the troop he continues, "Anything that be livin' lures them out of hiding. Small amounts of magic like yer flames ain't such a bad thing, but any more than that will bring 'em straight to us! Yer magic won't hurt them; it will just make them stronger!"

"How do we fight them if they attack us?" Bohdi asks.

"We don't fight—we run and hide!" Scallywag replies. "Tis our only way to surviving."

"Well, I don't like it! Where are the rest of your people? Maybe one of them can get us out of here quicker than you seem to be able to!" Daghan barks at him.

Slasher just glares at Daghan, "Well, if I knew that, we wouldn't be lost now would we, rocks for brains!"

"Did you just call me rocks for brains? You puny woglet. You need to understand one thing if nothing else. If you can't get us out of here, you are no good to me!" he says, leaning down in Slasher's face and poking him in the chest with his finger. "And if you're no good to me as a guide then I may as well make a meal out of you and your friends!" he snarks, showing off his fangs. "Because I'm starving!"

Slasher, Slade, and Scallywag all gulp at the same time as they back away. Suddenly a ruckus breaks out between the three of them as in their panic they start slapping and shoving each other, blaming each other, and calling each other names.

Asher, still carrying Sadie, looks on as the gollywoggles drop to the ground, kicking and biting each other and rolling back and forth in the dirt. "I doona think it's a good idea to be gettin' them all nervous and riled up like that, Daghan! Look at what it does to them!"

Daghan reaches down and grabs two of them by the scruff of their necks. "Okay, that's enough of that!" One quickly turns in his hand and bites down hard on his wrist. "*Snappin' garters!*" Daghan roars as he shakes the little creature roughly, its head whipping back and forth. "Don't do that again!" he growls.

Slasher and Scallywag continue to try to kick each other while Daghan holds them.

"*Stop it!* The both of you!" he says, giving the both of them a good hard shake. But the two don't listen. "I'm warning you!" he growls again. Still they don't listen as they continue to kick and slap at each other while dangling from his hands. Daghan, not knowing what else to do, knocks their heads together with a *thwack* in an attempt to calm them down. Instantly they stop and go limp in his hands. "That's better! Now, was that so hard?" he says with a smirk. Looking down, he sees Slade staring up at him as he puts the other two down. They both glare up at Daghan while rubbing their heads as they help Slade to his feet.

He looks down at the three small creatures as he takes a deep breath and blows it out slowly and then says, "Now, I would like to get topside as quickly as possible if you don't mind!"

Still rubbing the side of his head, Slasher gives Daghan a withering look, saying, "All right! All right already! No need to get yer undergarments in a twist! I'll get ye topside."

The three gollywoggles turn as one and start walking down another tunnel. Slasher looks back at the troop and says, "Well, what ye be waitin' for? We haven't got all night!"


Raine holds onto her human father's arm, hoping to steady him as they drop through the portal. She lands in a crouched position, quickly releasing him. Papa lands on his hands and knees, catching himself at the last second before falling flat on his face.

"Sorry about that, Dad. I had no idea what we might have dropped into the middle of and I had to be ready."

"That's okay, honey. It wasn't so bad." He stands, dusting his hands and knees off. "I'm just glad we didn't land in the top of a tree or something."

Looking around, Raine tries to remember what she was told about the forest. "Stay close, Dad. We are now in the middle of Nocturnal Forest on Mystic Mountain, and believe me it's named Mystic for a reason."

"Okay, you won't have to tell me twice." Squinting and blinking his eyes in the darkness, he tries to look around. "Man! It's really dark here! Is it always this dark at night? I mean, here in your world?" Peering into the night, he rubs his eyes, still trying to look around but is unable to see much. "Wow, saying that out loud sounded really weird! Your world," he says again, shaking his head, and squints, trying to see past the end of his nose. "Just plain weird!"

Raine watches him stumble in the darkness, groping around for something to hold on to, and chants:

> *"With my inner light,*
> *I grant thee fairy sight."*

"There, that should help!"

Blinking his eyes, he says, "Hey! I can see! Cool trick, Alece. I mean, Raine. Sorry, it's going to take me a little while, honey."

"It's okay, Dad. You don't have to be sorry. I'm just glad you've accepted everything so easily. Now stay close—we have to find Mom and Sadie." Standing still she reaches out with her mind, searching. "Nothing. I can't feel them. I can't find them!"

"You were doing that thing again with your mind, weren't you?" Out of nowhere he reaches over and touches the tip of one of her ears, gently squeezing it between thumb and forefinger. "Pointy ears, imagine that!

"Dad!" She swats at his hand. "What are you doing?"

"Sorry. I guess I just can't help myself. This is all so strange for me. You get that, right? I mean, you're still beautiful, but you're not the beautiful I'm used to."

"I know, Dad, but we have to put all that aside and concentrate on finding Sadie and Mom. They're in real danger here. This isn't like your world. Everything here is either made of magic or uses magic. You're not in your mountains anymore, Dad. You could all die here. Get it? Sadie's very powerful, but she doesn't know how to use her powers, well, other than playing with her toys and stuff."

"Yah, I get it. Okay, where do we start?"

"Let me try one more thing." She closes her eyes and reaches out again with her mind, this time searching for Rowan or Serena; she finds Rowan first. Opening her eyes, she sees him standing before her. "Rowan! Finally!"

Papa stands there, staring slack-jawed.

"Dad, this is Prince Rowan, Sadie's biological father. Rowan, this is my human father."

"Hello. You can call me Papa. That'll just make things easier." Reaching out, he takes hold of Rowan's hand and gives it a good shake. "Nice to meet you."

Rowan looks at his hand and then up at Raine, a frown forming on his handsome face. "This is no time to bring more humans into our world! We will be lucky to keep

Sadie safe without having to protect two humans as well! What were you thinking? Kieran himself hunts Sadie! You know as well as I do what that means—send the human back!"

"Now wait just a minute, Your Highness! I'm not going anywhere without my wife and granddaughter! I might be just a *human*, as you put it, but I assure you we *humans* have our talents too!"

Eyeing the large man before him, Rowan says, "You know nothing of our world! You have no magic! Without magic you have no way to protect yourself against what is coming! So please tell me, *human*, what *talents* do you possess?"

Papa, a stubborn look on his face, says, "I am not leaving without my wife and granddaughter!"

Raine watches the two men standing face to face, arms crossed over their chests, neither of them willing to budge. Not wanting the argument to go any further, she speaks up, "Prince Rowan, I will be responsible for his welfare and that of his wife. Now please, instead of standing around arguing we need to be searching for Sadie!"

"Very well, but understand this *human*," he says, pointing a finger in Papa's direction. "My only concern is the safety of my daughter!"

"Fine! Because the safety of my granddaughter and my wife are the only concerns I have! I'm glad we understand each other, *Your Almighty Highness*," Papa says, mocking him with an over exaggerated bow.

Rowan stands there looking at the impudent human and smiles inwardly. Without wanting to he finds himself liking this human male called Papa.

"Now that all of that is settled, have you been able to locate Sadie?" Raine asks.

"They are in the Cave of Dark Dreams, according to Lila. None of us has been able to sense her. Lila has been frantic and in pain since the separation," Rowan explains.

"What can we do? How will we find her?"

"All we can do for now is wait. They will have to come above ground to reach the falls. We need to be ready to intercept them before Kieran does."

# STRANGER THINGS HAVE HAPPENED

Following the gollywoggles through an endless labyrinth of twisting and turning passageways, trudging down tunnel after tunnel with no sign of their journey ever ending, has certainly taken its toll on everyone, except maybe the gollywoggles themselves.

Sadie has been listening to everyone's tummies taking turns growling and grumbling for the last hour or so. She is hungry and beyond tired of being underground, trudging on, second in line between Daghan and Asher ever since her ordeal with the slimy thing in the cave. She keeps wishing that this day would end, in a good way, that is, as she knows firsthand how it could end badly.

As the troop turns another corner Sadie catches sight of a small flame flickering in the distance. It begins to move toward them. She tugs on Daghan's hand and whispers, "Whose flame is that?" and points down the tunnel.

"Oh, what now? Asher, stay alert! It appears that we have company. You whisk Sadie and Baba out of here at the first sign of trouble, understand?"

"Got it, Daghan! First sign."

As the flame floats closer there is no sound of footfall or shuffling associated with it. There is no sound whatsoever, just the soft glow of a small flame floating in the air as it moves toward them. As it reaches the troop they all stand very still, waiting. Asher, holding Sadie and Baba's hands, watches the flame with wary eyes. The flame passes over the gollywoggles' heads as they watch, expressions of confusion and wonder on their faces. It passes first Daghan and then Asher as he pulls Sadie behind him. The little flame zips around him and stops directly in front of Sadie. Touching her shoulder it says, "Come."

Asher grabs Sadie and picks her up, saying, "Oh no, you doona have any say! She isna goin' anywhere with the likes of you! Now go on! Off with you now!" He waves the little flame away. It dodges his hand and begins jumping around in front of everyone saying,

*In these tunnels you can stay.*
*In these tunnels monsters play!*
*Follow me; I'm on your side.*
*Beware of where the monsters hide!"*

Daghan coming up behind the little flame asks, "Who are you, and why should we trust you?"

*"I am like the wind, as old as time*
*Hurry now do not lag behind*
*Trust me not if you wish,*
*become a meal, a tasty dish."*

The little flame darts around them, quickly retreating back down the tunnel and calling out, "Follow me. They are coming! They come for the child!"

At that precise moment the troop hears clicking sounds and scraping coming from the far end of the tunnel. Fear grips Sadie's insides, and she starts screaming, "Follow the flame! Follow the flame, Asher!"

Asher, at a loss for what else to do and not wanting to stick around to see what is coming their way, whips around and starts chasing after the flame, tightening his hold on Sadie as he runs down yet another long dark tunnel. Daghan and the rest of the troop follow suit, chasing Asher and Sadie and leaving the gollywoggles behind to fend for themselves.

They follow the little flame for a very long time, running down tunnel after tunnel, always turning left. Slowly the tunnels begin to steadily climb upward, becoming narrower, the ceiling closing in on them. Before long they are all crawling on their hands and knees, squeezing through small spaces. The faint sounds of clicking and scraping coming from behind them, driving them forward. When they finally reach the end of the tunnel the small flame hovers in front of a small opening for just a moment before winking out.

"Wait!" Daghan calls to it, but it's too late; the flame is gone. The opening is not big enough for all of them to fit through, and Daghan calls out to Bohdi, "I need you to shrink yourself and crawl through. We need to know what's out there."

Moving forward, Bohdi peeks through the opening. "I canna see a thin'. It's too dark out there!"

"That's why I need you to shrink yourself. That way you can fit through the opening."

"Why doona you shrink yourself?"

"Because I need to stay with Sadie in case those things catch up to us. Unless of course you want to stay and fight them when they show up."

"No! No, I'll take my chances out there. Back up, back up now! Give me some room."

Sadie watches curiously as a cyclone of twinkling lights wraps itself around Bohdi, swallowing him, spinning faster and then shrinking him down. As soon as it starts it's over and Bohdi emerges the size of a mouse.

"Don't you think that's a bit smaller than what is needed?" Daghan asks.

"No I do not! If somethin' is out there I doona want it seein' me!" Bohdi snarks.

"No need to get all snarky about it."

Sadie can now hear the clicking and scraping clearly and cries, "Hurry, Bohdi, please! Whatever those are, they're getting closer!"

Bohdi turns, runs to the opening, and dives into the hole, kicking his little feet as he squeezes through.


Still wandering around the mountainside, the assassin hears a noise just a couple of feet below him. Stopping, he listens; it sounds as if something's digging. On silent feet he creeps closer, just in time to see a tiny figure pop out of the ground. *An elf? The size of a mouse? Now what would an elf be doing popping out of the ground like that?* he wonders. Staying behind a tree he decides to wait.

Bohdi takes a couple of deep breaths as he looks around. It feels wonderful to be out of the tunnels and back in the forest. Looking around he doesn't see anything out of the ordinary. Turning back to the hole he calls, "All's clear. Come on out!"

"Get back!" Daghan yells so Bohdi can hear him as he cups his hands over his mouth and then whispers, "Wider!" Throwing his hands outward toward the small opening, he thinks, *Push*, with his mind. An explosion blows the end of the tunnel wide open, leaving only a thick cloud of dust standing between them and the forest as Daghan leads the troop out of the tunnels.

Once outside everyone sucks in the fresh air as they look around, the elves trying to figure out where they are. The roar of the falls is just an undertone in the distance but luckily not too far distant.

The assassin stands very still, his back pressed against the tree trunk, barely breathing. The explosion caught him off guard as he was stepping out from behind the tree. Now his only concern is not being caught. *Daghan*, he thinks with a sneer as he traces the scar under his left eye with his fingertip.

What he doesn't notice is the small elm beetle clinging to the side of the tree just above his head. With a smile on its face the beetle flies off in the direction of the falls whistling a long forgotten tune.

The assassin tilts his head back, looking up, his head swiveling from side to side. He's sure he just heard someone whistling, the tune an unfamiliar one.

Hearing the explosion, Rowan and Raine quickly reach out with their minds. Raine is the first to touch Sadie as she searches for her mother.

Daghan feels Rowan's touch, and then he is there standing before him. Raine and Papa appearing right behind him. *Raine*, he thinks and nods, surprised to see her. *I wonder where she's been for the last few years.*

Raine glances in Daghan's direction and then quickly looks away. She hasn't seen him since being assigned to Sadie. *He looks fit*, she thinks to herself.

Relief washes over Baba and Papa at the same time. Sadie squeals, "Papa!" as she takes off running straight into his outstretched arms.

"Munchkin!" He picks her up, spinning around, squeezing her tight. "I was so worried about the two of you. Are you both all right?"

"We're fine, Papa! Wait till I tell you everything that's happened."

Papa hugs her again, and looking over his shoulder Sadie sees someone who looks kind of like her aunt Alece but more fairy like and light blue. "Auntie Lece? Is that you?"

"It's me, kiddo. Come here and give me a big hug!"

Daghan, watching Raine, thinks, *Well, that answers that question.*

Putting Sadie down, Papa turns and gives his wife a big bear hug, whispering, "I've been so worried. Please don't do this ever again."

"No worries there. I'm good for a lifetime after this one!" she says, resting her head against Papa's chest.

Standing there watching the family reunion, Rowan finds himself a little put off. He knows he shouldn't, but he can't help feeling left out. The overwhelming desire he feels to hold his daughter becomes a physical ache inside his chest.

Holding Sadie's hand, Raine takes her to Rowan. He kneels down to be at eye level with Sadie. He simply stares at her for a moment and then says, "Your mother, sister, and I have been worried about you, little one. Lila has been crying nonstop since you entered the cave. Do you feel her now?" He reaches out and envelopes her small hands with his. "May I?" he asks, rubbing his thumbs across the backs of her hands he looks into her eyes.

Sadie nods her head up and down, never taking her eyes off the golden man, a man she now knows is her real father. "I can feel her in my heart," she says, touching her chest. "She's all better now. She's worried about you too, and she wants me to give you a hug. I know you're my real daddy, and I think you're very handsome."

Rowan's eyes mist over as he draws her into his arms. As he hugs her close to him the knot in his chest loosens just a bit.

"Well, well, what a pleasant sight to behold! Father and daughter reunited after all these years! It brings a mist to my eyes, truly it does." Kieran makes a show of wiping away fake tears from behind Rowan. "How wonderful it must be for you, Rowan, to find out that your precious daughter is alive and well. It must make you very angry. I know I am. That witch of a mother-in-law of yours thinks nothing of the lies she tells as long as it suits her purposes, eh Rowan?"

Angry because Kieran has ruined this precious moment with Sadie, Rowan slowly stands, and turning he puts Sadie behind him. Daghan and Raine walk to either side of Sadie. As Rowan steps toward Kieran, Raine steps around Sadie, putting her behind Daghan and herself. Baba, Papa, and the three elves close ranks behind her, sealing Sadie in the middle of all of them.

As Rowan walks toward Kieran, immense power rolls off of him in waves. "Why, Kieran, how unpleasant it is to see you again! I was hoping you were dead, but as usual you disappoint me. You do have a knack for showing up at the most inopportune times!" Rowan notices the tic by Kieran's right eye, a sign of hidden anger.

"Now, why don't you be a good ol' boy and go back to your fortress of black ice or wherever it is that you and your friends play these days." He gestures toward all of Kieran's minions. "Anywhere will do, just somewhere other than here in my presence! My daughter is of no concern to you. You have no business with her."

Kieran's facial features are drawn into a false expression of shock, and he places his hand over his heart in a mocking gesture, saying, "Really Rowan, your words truly wound me! I find myself at a loss for words, they cut me so deeply!" A small laugh escapes him and he looks away, unable to keep a straight face. "I apologize, Rowan. I actually thought I could get through that without laughing; my mistake. Now why don't we dispense with the idle chit-chat and you hand over the girl? *Now!*" he growls. Fighting to calm himself, he continues, "If you will just hand her over, I promise that my friends and I, as you so eloquently put it, will all leave peacefully. No harm, no foul. What do you say, hmmm?"

Power the likes of which no one present has ever seen before surrounds Rowan. His magic a living thing, the air around him snaps and crackles with it. Rowan looks to his left as an assassin saunters out from behind a tree. He also takes note of several goblins, two yaksha, a couple of ogres, and several other strange-looking fae that seem to be a mix of more than one type.

"I say that your comment just proves to me that you are still the lack-wit that you always were, Kieran. You and your puny minions are no match for me, and you know it."

"True! Well, it would be true except for one tiny element. It would seem that you have forgotten where we are!" Saying this he shouts, "Now!"

Instantly, bush soldiers spring from the ground. Twisted thorny vines growing upward out of the ground quickly forming into tall humanoid shapes, the mindless creatures only doing what they are told by the one who wields power over them. They wrap themselves around the nearest victim, their poison already dripping from the tips of their thorns. Their poison renders their victims unconscious so they can be dragged underground, the hapless victim's magic and life essence slowly absorbed over time.

Instantly the situation unfolds into chaos. In a flash Asher grabs Sadie and Baba, transporting them out of the way safely.

Finn summons Ryder as he's wrapped in a tangle of thorny branches from behind. His arms are pinned to his sides as the bush soldier embraces him, its thorns piercing his flesh. The wolverine appears and immediately starts tearing the branches off Finn, snapping them in half with his powerful jaws and then stomping them into bits and pieces. But he is too late—as he's freed, Finn collapses to the ground, unconscious. Ryder gently picks him up in his massive jaws and sprints away, following Asher's trail of magic.

The branches of the bush soldiers have no effect on Raine as they pass right through her. Elemental fairies are unaffected by the magic of other's unless they are caught completely off guard. Calling on the elements, she draws moisture from the air to form an ice axe. The ice axe instantly freezes anything it comes into contact with, allowing Raine to shatter it into tiny frosty bits. She watches in horror as Papa is encased in the thorny embrace of a bush soldier. It immediately begins to slip back under the ground, taking him with it. She rushes to where her father is and begins hacking at the thorny branches freeing him. As Papa lies at her feet, unconscious, she casts a spell, wrapping him in a crystalline cocoon that the dark fae can neither transport nor penetrate and then moves on to find Daghan.

Rowan watches the chaos around him as it plays out quickly. He is unconcerned, because Kieran's tricks are merely that—tricks.

Rowan spreads his arms wide and brings his hands together with a loud clap, sending out a shock wave and instantly turning the bush soldiers into dust while simultaneously scattering Kieran's minions to the farthest reaches of the forest.

Before Kieran can even react they are all gone, leaving Kieran to stand alone thwarted and embarrassed. Throwing his head back he screams into the night, "Rowan! The child is mine! You can hide, but you cannot leave! I will find her!"

# THE COUP DE REGROUP

Not wanting to go directly to the falls and possibly alert Kieran to the presence of the last remaining portal, Rowan and the rest of the troop meet up with Asher, Baba, Sadie, Finn, and Ryder, appearing under a ledge surrounded by tall trees and bushes some distance away from the falls.

"Is everyone well?" Rowan asks.

Raine, crouched beside a sleeping Papa, looks from him to the sleeping form of Finn. "All except these two. Is there anything you can do to wake them?"

"Unfortunately, no. I'm afraid it will just have to wear off naturally. I doubt that it will take much time though. Without the continual dose of poison from the bush soldiers it should wear off fairly quickly."

"I hope so. It probably won't take Kieran long to track us," Asher remarks.

"I cast a spell leaving several trails for him to follow, and that should allow us the time we need," Rowan assures them all.

Suddenly Sadie gets that tingly feeling at the nape of her neck again. She now knows that it is a warning sign she gets whenever the huge wolf is close. She scans the area but is unable to see much due to the dense bushes and trees that surround them.

Baba hasn't said much the entire trip through the forest because she didn't want to be a distraction. She suddenly finds herself overwhelmed with the stress and fear she has been desperately trying to keep at bay all night. Holding her husband's head in her lap and looking down into his sleeping face, she is unable to hold it in any longer. She looks up and glances at all of those around her and feels that it is suddenly all too bizarre.

Quietly she asks, "What are we going to do?" All eyes turn to her. "I mean really, look at us. We're all huddled in a circle, hiding under a ledge. This is all just so crazy!" Looking from Rowan to Daghan to Raine, her focus settles on Raine, and she continues. "Alece, is that really you? What's going on? Why do you look like that? I didn't even recognize you at first!"

With all that had been happening, no one had gotten the chance to tell Baba about who Alece really is. Even Sadie had forgotten to mention it in all the excitement.

"Oh, Mom, I'm so sorry. I didn't mean for you to find out this way. There was no time to talk with you before everything started happening." She reaches over to her human mother, taking her hand and giving it a gentle squeeze. Sadie watches quietly, a little ashamed for not telling Baba about Auntie Alece being a fairy named Raine.

"Talk to me about what? Why do you look like that, Alece? I don't understand what's happening!" Baba says, her voice taking on a higher pitch. "Why are your hands so cold, and why is your skin blue? And what's with the pointy ears and your silvery white hair?" Pulling her hand loose from her daughter, she reaches out and caresses the tip of her ear.

"It feels so real." She touches Raine's hair and looks at her, her eyes starting to mist over. "Alece?"

"Mom, it's okay. Don't cry. Everything will be fine. Nothing of real importance has changed. You, Dad, Sadie and I, all of us will be just fine. I promise you."

"I know we will but I want to know why you look like that, Alece."

Unable to keep quiet any longer, Sadie says, "Because Auntie Alece is really a fairy like me, Baba. The queen, my other grandma, sent her to watch over me while I was growing up. Oh yah, her real name is Raine; cool, huh?"

"Sadie, you don't just blurt it out like that! Mom, look at me! I'm still me."

Baba sat there stunned, her eyes wide. Shock and disbelief are written all over her face. "But I remember being pregnant, giving birth to you, holding you in my arms afterward. This can't be true!" Looking all around, she notices that everyone has been paying rapt attention to what was being said. As she looks from one to the next they all glance away except Rowan. "Is this true?" she asks him. "Why didn't you tell me when we were talking? Couldn't you have prepared me for this? Given me some sort of warning?"

Rowan looks her straight in the eyes, telling her, "I give you my word—I did not know at the time. I only found out just after you left when Lila told us what Aurelia had told the girls."

Seeing the expression on Baba's face, Sadie snuggles up to her, saying, "I'm sorry I forgot to tell you, Baba. I'm so sorry."

Clutching Sadie close to her she says, "So you're telling me that you're not my real daughter. That all of my memories of you before Sadie was born are a lie. Is that what you're saying?" Raine looks on helplessly.

"None of it is true?" she asks quietly, her eyes misting over. Looking down at her lap she continues, "How can that be possible?" She whispers more to herself than those around her.

Looking back up at Raine she says, "You're twenty-three years old. You were fifteen when Sadie was born. I have fifteen years of memories, memories of you learning to walk and talk, you learning to ride a bike, the two of us talking about life and boys. We took trips together and did crazy things that no one else would do except you and I. We watched shows and movies, laughing together when no one else did, and you're telling me that none of that's real!"

Suddenly her eyes widen. "The queen!" she says with a slight sneer. "She did this to me, didn't she? She put all those memories, all of those lies in my brain, didn't she?" Her eyes grow even wider as she hisses, "She messed with my mind!"

Baba is quite suddenly very angry. "What gave her the right? Just who does she think she is, messing with my mind like that?" Looking at Rowan and Raine she asks, "Where is she? Why isn't she here with us?" Raine looks over at Rowan helplessly, not knowing how to answer.

"You call her or summon her or whatever it is you do to contact her. Do it right now, and you tell her I said to fix this mess, all of it! I want to go home! Now!"

At this point Baba is so angry that it's almost choking her. "Well? Why are the two of you just sitting there looking at me as if I've lost my mind? Call that retched queen of yours and have her fix this. *Now!*"

"Mom, we can't! She's our queen. You have to understand—we don't have the right to question what she does. We just do as she commands. I know that you're upset, and you have every right to be, but please understand—we need to deal with all of this later. Right now we have to get Sadie home, where we can protect her from Kieran. Sadie's safety is what matters now! That is all that matters right now. Can't we talk about all of this later with Dad when we get home?"

Looking down at Sadie, Baba gives her a squeeze and then says, "You're right, of course. I'm sorry for losing control. I guess all the stress and then seeing you looking like that was just too much for me and I snapped. I didn't mean to lose sight of the fact that *my granddaughter's* safety comes first." This last part was said pinning Rowan with a look that said, "I dare you to correct me about Sadie being *my granddaughter.*"

"Mom, it's okay. Look, Dad's starting to come around."

Just then Papa opens his eyes and looks up at his wife. Smiling up at her, he says, "Hi honey, what did I miss?" Baba helps him to a sitting position, and he looks around, asking, "Where are we?"

"We are in an enclosed outcropping of rock and trees some distance away from the falls," Rowan tells him. "Your mate has just found out that Raine is not who she thinks she is. She did not take it well, as you might imagine."

"Thanks for bringing me up to speed on all of that, sport." He turns to his wife and asks, "Are you okay?"

"We'll have time to talk later. For now we need figure out how we're going to get all of us home."

Yawning rather loudly as he stretches his arms and legs Finn reaches up to scratch the side of his head as he sits up and looks around. Shaking his head to clear the cobwebs, he asks, "What did I miss? I knew I was a goner when I felt the first sting on the back of my leg. Was it a good fight? I'll bet you had ol' Kieran runnin' with his tail between his legs. Didn't you, Rowan!"

Bohdi speaks up before Rowan can answer, "No, we were the ones who left. Although it was over before it actually became a fight."

"What we need now is a plan to lure Kieran away from the falls so that Raine and I can get Sadie and the two humans back to their world," Daghan says, looking around at everyone. "Anyone have any good ideas on how to accomplish that? I'm open for a discussion."

Baba speaks up again, "What were all those creepy things with Kieran anyway? The two tall ones with the white translucent skin, long black hair, and dark red eyes remind me of a vampire."

"They're called yaksha. I guess they are something similar to a vampire. They're wraith-like, cannibalistic fae that hunt the wilderness in search of lone travelers or small troops of two or three. They like to play with their food—they chase their victims for a while, taunting them, scaring them beyond reason. They feed off their fear first then run them to ground, and when they're finally too tired to go on, they suck out their life force and magic, leaving them to exist as an empty shell of what they once were. Like a zombie, I guess, for lack of a better word."

Wide-eyed, Baba hugs Sadie closer to her. She covers Sadie's ears as she asks in a whisper, "Those things are hunting Sadie too? What about all the other ones? Do they *all* suck people dry?"

"No Mom, they don't all suck people dry," Raine says, smiling.

"Anyway, getting back on track, how are we going to lead Kieran as well as all his minions away from the falls? Suggestions anyone?" Daghan asks.

Speaking up, Asher says, "Well, my brothers and I could create a couple of distractions to get his attention and then lead him and whoever is with him on a wild goose chase."

"That's good. I'm sure we'll need all of your special talents before this night is over, Asher."

Rowan looks at everyone in the troop and says, "Let us get down to business. I believe we are almost out of time."

# TRICKS OF THE TRADE

Kieran and his minions gather in a small clearing, regrouping after their long journeys back from the outer edges of the forest as well as tracking all of Rowan's false trails. They all realize that they have just wasted a lot of valuable time traveling and searching. "Did any of you find anything? Any clues to where they have gone?" Kieran asks.

"No, my lord," one of the yaksha reply in a deep chilling voice that mists the air around them. "It would seem that the prince tricked all of us."

"So it would seem, but why are they here in this part of the forest? That is the question we need to be asking ourselves," Kieran remarks. "I have closed the portals and posted guards at all of them. There is nowhere for them to go. So why are they here? And what does Raine have to do with all of this? I have not seen or heard anything about her in quite some time. Interesting!"

"What are they doing traveling with two humans? What purpose do the humans serve?" a goblin grouches. He brightens as an afterthought occurs to him. "Maybe they are food for their journey? Can we eat them?" he asks hopefully.

Kieran starts to respond, "I'm not sure. What? Food?" He looks at the goblin. "Eat them? Well, I suppose you could. Yes, yes, you may eat them. What do I care what you eat!" As he starts to pace he quickly forgets about the goblin. "Now I know that the human female traveled here with the young princess. I do not know who the human male is or why he is here. But the humans do not matter anyway. All that matters is the princess. She is to be *my heir*. And being *my heir* I want her found and captured but unharmed. Do you all understand me? Unharmed!"

A round of yeses runs through the band of dark fae. Some have disappointed looks on their faces. The little princess's power would greatly enhance their own if they were allowed to feed on her.

Changing his line of thought Kieran asks, "Have any of you seen Gothock?"

Lumbering slowly through the forest, his forked tongue flicking in and out, Gothock is tracking something or someone that he thinks will make a nice meal. He's been following his tongue for quite some time now when suddenly he stops and sniffs the air and his tongue flicks in and out. His beady black eyes scan the darkness as his massive head slowly swings from side to side. He can't see or hear very well, but it doesn't matter. His sense of smell and his excellent sense of taste guide him, and right now those senses are on alert. His long forked tongue silently licks the air, tasting his prey. He doesn't recognize the scent or the taste, but it's moving in his direction, getting closer. The amount of slime dripping from his mouth increases with the anticipation of a meal, and he hunkers down and waits patiently for his prey.

Seemingly oblivious to their surroundings, a band of gollywoggles make their way toward Gothock. Slasher, Slade, and Scallywag have joined up with three other gollywoggles. All of them are out searching for Sadie. As they're walking each one snuffles the air every few feet. Gollywoggles have a very good sense of smell as well as impeccable hearing and eyesight.

Snuffling the air, Scallywag is the first to catch Sadie's scent. Unfortunately he also catches a faint whiff of something else. "Oye!" Sniffing around he says, "Do ye smell that? It smells like somethin' has died somewheres out in the forest."

"Well, o' course it smells that way out there!" Slasher snarks. "Tis probably just some soulless cur up and walkin' around, tis all. The forest be full o' them this time o' night," he says while peering into the darkness.

"Nooo." He drags the word out and sniffs the air again. "Not dead exactly. Just somethin' that smells real bad like 'em."

"Well, what do ye think is out there, Scallywag? If'n it ain't dead, what is it?" Slade asks.

"Well, I don't rightly know! I just knows that it smells rotten but not our forests kind o' rotten!" he snaps. "If'n yer wantin' ta be figurin' it out, start sniffin'!"

Now all the gollywoggles start sniffing the air, walking around in tight little circles. Finally Slasher says, "I don't rightly know what that smell is, but the princess be this way." He points over his shoulder. "I says we go this way, find the princess, en avoid that smell altogether. What say the rest of ye?"

"Aye, aye, aye!" they say as each of their big round heads bob up and down. "Tis settled then! Let us be off. We're waistin' time sniffin' around here."

Skirting the bad smell, they head in the opposite direction. Quietly creeping through the forest they follow Sadie's scent.

Meanwhile, Gothock has resumed lumbering through the forest in pursuit of the gollywoggles. Licking the air, tasting each one, he is sure one of them will make a tasty meal.

# IT'S BEST TO DUCK WHEN YOU PLUCK

"Are you sure we need to do this, Asher? Are you sure this will work when we need it to?" Bohdi asks. "She isna gonna like it, and I really doona blame her!"

I'm tellin' you it will work. It's not as if I'm askin' for a fist full, I'm just askin' for two! Or three! No more than four, at most," he says, shrugging sheepishly.

"Four! How many tail feathers do you think she has? This better work, Asher!" Bohdi growls. Grudgingly he summons Hooty. His beautiful blue-eyed owl appears, rustling her feathers, stretching out her left wing, and gently nibbling at the underside with her beak. Engrossed in grooming herself, she doesn't notice Bohdi reach around behind her until it's too late. He grabs a few tail feathers and yanks down hard on them, plucking them out in one swift motion as he takes off running.

Hooty's head snaps up from under her wing. Her body stiff and her head stretched skyward, she screeches into the night. She takes off after Bohdi, swooping down on him like he's a meal, her feet stretched out before her. She lands on top of him with such force that it pushes him face first into the ground. As he skids to a halt she begins pecking at his head and shoulders. She bites him once for each feather he took and then a couple more times to teach him a lesson. When she's done she flies up into a tree, watching the troop from deep within its branches.

Peeling himself out of the ground, he sits back on his heels. He looks down at the impression of his body in the ground and begins brushing the dirt from his face. Rubbing and massaging the back of his head and shoulders, he pins Asher with an icy stare. "Dad-nab-it Asher! Next time you're doin' the pluckin'! This stupid idea of yours better work or I'll be bitin' you!"

Everyone, having prepared for the deafening screech ahead of time, continues to hold their ears until the sound rolls off into the distance. Even tightly covering their ears wasn't enough to completely block the effects of her screech. They all feel woozy, and their ears still ring. One by one they drop their hands and shake their head. "*Wow! That was loud!*" Sadie yells, her voice loud due to the ringing in her ears.

Rowan eyes the poor owl up in the tree, feeling sorry for it. "I'll bet that screech comes in handy at times. Hopefully you don't have to do that every time to make it happen."

Rubbing his head and the back of his neck, Bohdi says, "No, I doona have to and yes it does, but it doesna bother me like it does everyone else."

Seeing that the owl has alighted onto a lower branch, he gives Hooty a wide berth. The major stink-eye that she's giving him tells Bohdi that all is not forgiven. He walks up to the rest of the troop. "I'm tellin' you right now, Asher, I willna ever do that again!" he says as he hands him a feather. He then gives one to Finn and one to Sadie. He stashes the fourth one in a pocket on the inside of his coat.

"She really hit you hard!" Finn says, chuckling. "I'll bet there's an imprint of your face back there in the dirt where she landed on you. Pushed your face right into it, she did!" he says, chuckling again.

"I'm real glad you find it so amusing, Finn! I'll try to remember that the next time I sneeze around you! So you just keep on laughin'."

At that comment Finn sobers; suddenly he doesn't find it funny anymore.

Hearing a noise directly behind her Sadie jumps as she turns around and then squeals, "Papa! Something's behind me in the bushes!"

Rowan's on his feet and beside Sadie in a flash, moving so quickly no one even saw him. Reaching into the bushes he grabs ahold of something squirmy and drags it out, throwing it into the middle of their circle.

Sadie, having climbed into her Papa's lap after jumping up, says, "Hey, look everyone. It's Scallywag! Where's Slasher and Slade?"

Rowan looks at the gollywoggle, asking, "You know him?"

"Sure. He's one of the gollywoggles that were supposed to help us get out of the tunnels. They didn't do a very good job of it though."

Scallywag stands up massaging his throat and looks toward the bushes, calling out, "Oye, come on now, out with ye! All of ye, out of the bushes."

Slasher and Slade crawl through the opening first followed by three more gollywoggles. Standing, they all look around. Slasher pokes all three of the new ones, pointing, and says, "See! I told ye, humans!" Realizing that he said *humans* and not *human* he points an accusing finger at Papa, asking, "And just where be you from?"

Daghan speaks up. "Never mind that. How did you get here? Better yet, how did you find us? And who are they?" he says, pointing to the other gollywoggles.

"We found ye by followin' our noses!" Slasher says, pointing to his. "And they be friends of ours. This here's Striker, that one there is Snorbert, and that one over there be Kevin. I'd be remiss in me duties if I didn't tell ye to be givin' that one there a wide berth!" Slasher whispers conspiratorially. "He be a bit of a long shot. Cuz he has such a strange name en all! Very unperdictable! So don't get the bloke all riled up, savvy?"

Daghan quickly looks Kevin up and down, thinking he does look a bit stranger than the rest.

He turns to Rowan. "I believe it's time to move out. We can use these little guys as bait," he says as a plan forms in his mind. "If I may suggest, we can send Asher and his brothers out in the opposite direction from Raine and me. You can take the gollywoggles with you. Use them as a distraction if you need to. What do you think?"

Rowan nods his head up and down, and unable to think of a better idea, he agrees. "I will keep in constant contact with Sadie. I will not be at peace until she finally slips through the portal." He looks around and asks, "Does everyone know their part in this? If you have any questions ask now!"

Scallywag speaks up, "What did he mean, use us as a distraction?"

# EVERYTHING GOES WILLY-NILLY

Wishing each other good luck and saying their good-byes all around the small troop breaks off into three smaller troops.

Daghan and Raine take Papa, Baba, and Sadie and head for the falls.

Asher and Finn mount their pets. Bohdi shrinks himself and sullenly climbs onto Finn's shoulder, Hooty having refused to allow him to ride on her. They head off in a direction diagonal from that of Daghan and Raine, heading straight for where they last saw Kieran.

Rowan heads away from Sadie, intending to slowly climb upward and then circle around and double back to the falls. The band of six gollywoggles following in his wake, talking nonstop. As he's walking, Rowan spells false trails in all directions, making them crisscross at times, mixing in a few odd smells and even leaving footprints on some of them as proof of their passage.

"What is taking so long?" Ezra asks, clearly irritated. "Zara! Did you hear what I asked? What is wrong with you? You've been occupied elsewhere in your mind since we last spoke with our master."

Zara, not wanting to reveal her true thoughts, shrugs and then says, "I have been thinking about our new potions. What will happen if they do not work? I do not want a repeat of earlier this night. Being squeezed like that was very unpleasant."

"Don't worry—all will work out just fine. I took special care in the mixing of them. Besides, now that you brought it up, I will tell you that I have prepared a potion for us. Just in case something does go wrong."

"Really? What does it do? Will it save us from our master's wrath if he is displeased with what we made for him?"

"That, my dear friend, is the truly devious part." Pulling an orb from her personal sack, she holds it out for Zara. "This little beauty will erase one's memories, leaving their mind blank. All that needs to be done is to toss it at their feet hard enough to break it; then we run. The gas will spread several feet around them, so do not go through it while close to them."

Zara tries to hand it back to her. "No, you keep that one for yourself. We don't yet know how this night will play out."

"I am touched that you thought of me. You are a good and true friend, Ezra."

"How nice. Another touching, nauseating moment that I am forced to witness this night," Kieran drawls from behind them.

They both jump at the intrusion. "Master!" Ezra exclaims, unsure of how long he has been there. "You grace us with your presence yet again in one night. We've been waiting for your instructions."

"We have been keeping watch for you and have seen no one. Well, no one except for that one assassin, but that was earlier," Zara rambles as Ezra cuts her a sideways glance.

Kieran looks from one to the other, "Stop your babbling! Now, do you know where the queen's man is escorting the young princess to? There has to be a reason that they are climbing this mountain at night. Well, do you?"

Ezra and Zara think for a moment, their blank expressions answer enough for Kieran. "Never mind. Just keep an eye out for them and be ready if you see them. I want this skirmish over with as quickly as possible."

"Yes, master," they answer in unison. But they are speaking to thin air; Kieran is already gone.

Meeting up with his minions, Kieran has decided to summon the dead, raising all of them to hunt for Sadie. "My decision is not up for debate. I'm raising the dead, and all of you will just have to deal with them. Between the dead and all of you searching for her we ought to find her fairly quickly."

"But sire, the dead will also turn on us," a goblin whines.

"That's right—snacks is what we'll be," another chimes in as a few others voice their concerns as well.

"They do not take sides; they only hunt for food," one of the yaksha comments, stating the obvious in a cold, chilling voice.

"I am quite sure they will not be a problem for you, my friend, not with your hunting skills. The rest of you stop your whining and stay out of their way! Now cease your sniveling all of you! I need to concentrate."

Knowing that all eyes are upon him, Kieran does not disappoint them. With an exhibition of sweeping hand gestures and a deep booming voice so that all can hear him he begins his chant:

> *"From under the ground I summon you this night,*
> *Your mangled bodies a frightful sight,*
> *Twisted bones and putrid flesh,*
> *The stench of rot upon your breath.*
> *I need an army of undead slaves.*
> *Arise my pets from your wormy graves.*
> *Search the forest for the one I seek.*
> *Feast upon the unsuspecting and the meek."*

Magic explodes outward from Kieran in waves, rolling through the forest. They can hear the sounds of scraping, twigs snapping, and rocks rolling as the dead unearth themselves all around them.

Pleased with himself, Kieran claps his hands together as a smile splits his dark features. "Well, I would say from the sounds around us that my spell was a huge success, wouldn't you?" Looking at all of the faces around him, he smiles. The fear in their eyes excites him. "Well, don't just stand there. Go! Search! I want my heir found before daybreak! When you find her bring her straight to me, no delays!"

The troop disbands, breaking off into smaller parties of two and three, each warily heading in different directions.

After riding at breakneck speed, the elves finally slow to a walk. The brothers have traveled quite a distance in a very short time since leaving the others.

"Start looking around for signs of which way they went," Asher says.

Looking at the forest floor while reaching out with their senses, the three brothers search in an ever-widening circular pattern, trying not to miss any sign. Their pets alternate sniffing the ground and the air. Ryder and Arlo catch the scent of decay at the same time. Shaking their heads and snorting, they alert their riders.

As the elves pick up the scent Bohdi asks, "What in all of Otherworld could be stinkin' up our forest like this?"

Finn wraps a bandana around his nose and spells it to smell like his favorite flower to help hide the stench of putrid flesh that hangs in the air. Bohdi does the same. "I have never in all of my life known of a time that our forest has smelled like this. Have you, Asher?"

Asher comes up alongside Finn and Bohdi. Asher has followed Finn's lead and wrapped a bandana around his face. "No! Never! It must be somethin' Kieran's done to it! Maybe he's tryin' to force us out of the forest by stinkin' it up!"

"Well, I doona know about the two of you, but if that's his plan it's workin' on me!" Bohdi snarks as he tries to summon Hooty again. "Blasted bird! Because of you and your stupid idea, Asher, my pet willna come when I summon her. She's still mad at me for pluckin' those feathers. Now I'm stuck in this awful stink with the two of you!"

"Listen!" Asher says, holding up one hand. "Do you hear that?" All around them the brothers can now hear wheezing and gurgling. Asher and Finn bring their pets closer together, facing in opposite directions. "We're surrounded!" Finn whispers.

"Surrounded by the rotting corpses of dead wolves! Look!" Bohdi points as one of the creatures steps into the light of the full moon.

What was once a mighty wolf is now the shrunken, rotting corpse of a canine, its eyes now white, sightless, glowing orbs, swollen and bulging from their sockets. Its skull is half exposed, with most of its fur already gone. Lowering its head, ooze and slime drips from between its teeth. It snaps its jaws at them, gurgling as it inches forward on stiff legs, what's left of the hair on its back bristling.

The wolf, bathed in moonlight, never completely leaves their sight, and as the three elves scan the darkness between the trees as one by one a different set of glowing, eerie white eyes blink into focus. Twigs snap as the undead creatures slowly creep toward them. The wheezing and gurgling sounds grow louder as the wolves press forward, tightening their circle around the elves. Their numbers are terrifying.

"Asher, what do you suggest we do?" Finn whispers.

"I say we pull our weapons and fight!" he bellows.

The wolves sprint forward all at once, their jaws snapping, black ooze dripping from their mouths. Wheezing and gurgling sounds mix with guttural barking as they lunge at the elves in mass from all sides.


"Do we have to climb straight up, Daghan?" Sadie complains for the fourth time.

"Yes, straight up!" he rasps in a choking voice. "You're choking me again, Sadie!" She loosens her grip just a bit. "Besides, what are you complaining about? You're riding on my back! I'm the one doing all the climbing!"

"I'm scared! What if you fall? I'll go down with you, you know!"

"Oh, Sadie, quit giving him such a hard time," Raine says sweetly. "He would never let you fall. Isn't that right, Daghan?" Before he can answer she continues, "Because after all, you're a big strong warrior. The queen's mightiest! If one can believe all the gossip." she says in a velvety voice dripping with sarcasm.

"Have I done something to upset you? Or are you just naturally snarky?" Daghan puffs, glancing sideways at her as he hefts himself and Sadie up and over another rock ledge. As Raine starts to speak Daghan interrupts, "I'm gonna go with *snarky* because that is one part of the gossip being spread throughout the realms that I personally know to be true!" Leaping across her path to grab the ledge above her, he flicks dirt in her face with his foot as he pushes off to swing up and over the ledge.

Rearing back, she closes her eyes to avoid the dirt. She shakes her head and gives a little cough as she glares up at the ledge.

Setting Sadie aside for the moment he leans back over the ledge, extending his arm downward. "May I be of service, my lady? Being a mighty warrior and all, it is my duty to help when and where I can."

As she reaches up Raine smiles sweetly. "How kind of you, Daghan," she says, batting her eyes coyly.

Eyeing her suspiciously, Daghan still doesn't see it coming until it's too late. Reaching up, Raine grasps his hand, freezing his arm all the way to his shoulder. Letting go of Daghan and the cliff, she floats free from the mountainside, giving him an icy stare as she rises above him. "I'm quite capable of rising above you all on my own," she says with a smirk and a wink as she floats past him.

Daghan looks at his frozen arm. "Funny, Raine! Very funny." He looks at Sadie. "I suppose you're gonna take her side in all of this?"

"No. I think you're both acting like little kids. And I mean little kids, as in much younger than me!" she snarks as she looks around. "Great, just great!" Throwing her head back she yells, "Thanks a lot, Auntie. I mean Raine. Now how am I supposed to get up there—you froze his arm!"

Just then Papa lifts himself up onto the ledge and looking back over the side reaches down to help Baba over. They both notice Daghan's arm and smile.

Sadie looks at her grandparents and puts her hands on her hips, saying, "It's not funny, you know. Daghan did something to make Raine mad, and she froze his arm!" At this remark they both start laughing. "Now how is he supposed to carry me?"

"Although I am humbled by your show of concern for me, Princess," he says sarcastically. "There's no need to worry; it's already wearing off. See?" He flexes his arm. "Snarky, I tell you! Just plain snarky!"

"Has Raine always been like this with you?" Baba asks. "Because I've never seen her act like this before."

From above they hear a miffed voice call out, "That's because you've never seen me around him before!"

"I'll take that as a yes!" Papa chuckles.

"I'm glad you both find it so amusing. Now can we continue climbing, I would like this night to be over as soon as possible if you don't mind."

"That makes two of us!" Raine yells from somewhere above.

Lifting Sadie onto his back once again, Daghan leaps up to catch hold of a small ledge.

"Do you smell that?" Sadie asks as she pinches her nose with one hand while trying to hang on.

"Oh, man! What is that horrible smell? Something must have died close by!" Daghan replies.

Just below them they both hear coughing and comments drifting up from Baba and Papa.

Looking up Daghan calls to Raine, "You could have warned us about the stench!"

The lofty voice from above calls down, "It just drifted up out of nowhere all of a sudden, Daghan, so naturally I thought it was you. I've seen nothing up here that could be the cause of it."

Unexpectedly, a hoard of undead squirrels jump to the edge of the tree branches, planning to ambush them. The slimy, oozing creatures appear all around them. Daghan pulls Sadie to the front of him, showing her how he wants her to hang on. "Close your eyes if you don't want to see them."

Raine appears next to Daghan and Sadie with an arm full pinecones, their quarrel forgotten for the time being. She whispers an enchantment, and the pinecones begin to glow and multiply as she puts them down on the ledge. Daghan arches a brow in question.

"What? We can use these like grenades. You know the only way to kill these things is to burn them or cut off their heads. I just thought this would be a fun and easy way to get rid of a pest problem."

Baba and Papa scramble onto the ledge. "What's happening? Where'd all the smelly zombie squirrels come from?" Papa asks.

Daghan starts collecting pinecones, placing them in the hidden pockets of his uniform. "Apparently Kieran fancies himself a necromancer now. It seems he has risen the dead, all of the dead. Probably to help him search for Sadie and to hopefully eliminate a few of us as well. Don't let them bite you!"

Sadie hangs on tightly as Daghan stuffs more pinecones into his outfit. They seem to just disappear once inside his pockets. "Can I throw some of those at the squirrels, Daghan? I'm not afraid of them. I already had one try to bite my hand. I think it would be fun to blow them up. After all, they're already dead. It's not like I'll be killing them!"

"I'm sure you'll get your chance, Princess, because I think they're going to attack. Everyone arm themselves!"

Hurrying, Raine hands several to Baba and Papa, keeping a close eye on the squirrels and saying, "Just get them as close as possible. I've spelled the pinecones to ignite and throw out sparks as soon as they leave our hands. They will explode on impact. The important thing is that we stay together. Don't let them separate us, okay?"

"Got it!" Papa looks at Baba. "Well, this oughta be fun; stay close!"

Daghan swings Sadie onto his back again, having decided that they should all stand back to back, keeping Sadie surrounded and shielded by their bodies. "You can throw the pinecones over my shoulders, but do not slide off my back, understood?"

"I won't, Daghan. I'll stay put." As she says this the squirrels start chattering, squeaking, and wheezing all around them. Daghan and Raine both yell, "*Now!*" The five of them start lobbing pinecones in all directions. The squirrels retreat just a bit at first as some are blown apart and others catch fire, spreading the flames from themselves to others as they scamper away.

Sadie and Baba hoot and holler as they pitch their bombs at the squirrels. "Take that! You smelly things!" Sadie yells. "Bite this! You slimy bag of bones!"

Raine quickly realizes that they are far outnumbered. The squirrels keep coming, a never-ending surge of little rotting corpses. Step by step the creatures gain more ground, shrinking the distance between them and the troop. "Daghan, they're getting closer. There are just too many of them. Our arms will tire soon, way before we can kill them all," she says as she throws a couple more bombs.

"I can see that! You may have to take Sadie on your own while I hold them off."

"No! I won't leave my parents. But I have an idea. Sadie, hang on tight to Daghan. It's going to get really windy. Stay low to the ground and hang on to whatever you can," she calls to her parents. Gathering her magic she floats away from the ledge. Twinkling lights begin to flow around her as the wind picks up.

Becoming stronger, the wind whips through the trees, snapping the branches back and forth and flinging the small rotting creatures from their limbs. She calls for the wind to blow stronger, and hurricane force gales rip through the trees. Baba and Papa are now on the ground with their backs to the cliff, covering their faces with their arms as the wind kicks sand and small rocks up into the air.

As squirrels lunge at the troop the wind snatches them in midair, whipping them away before they can land on their prey. "It's working!" Daghan yells above the roar of the wind.

Raine searches the surrounding trees. She scans the cliff face and the upper ledges as best she can. "I don't see any more squirrels for now. I think it's safe to resume our climb."

The wind dies down, and the five of them begin climbing again.


"Do ye mind tellin' me where we are goin', yer grace?" Slasher asks again, still waiting for an answer.

Rowan ignores the gollywoggle just as he had each time before. He continues to conjure false trails and shadow people, throwing them out indiscriminately as he goes. Hoping to keep Kieran and his minions busy searching in all the wrong places.

"Oye, excuse me, yer grace. I don't mean to be disturbin' ye, bein's that I know yer busy an all, but do ye smell that awful stench? It seems to have just snuck up on us all of a sudden like," Scallywag asks as he sniffs the air while trailing behind Rowan.

Rowan stops, and the small creature runs into his backside. Turning around, he looks down and arches an eyebrow.

Looking up at Rowan, the gollywoggle takes a step back. Scallywag takes this as a positive sign and continues to press forward. "'Tis a powerful rot to be sure, yer grace. Never before have I smelled such an odorous presence in the forest!" he says while skimming the darkness with a wary eye.

"I will have to agree with you on this matter. I myself have never experienced such a putrid stench before." Using his fairy sight, he peers into the darkness, searching the trees and bushes for movement. "Nothing, just the overpowering stench of rotting flesh. This is Kieran's doing. I'm sure of that! But to what end?" he muses.

"There, yer grace!" One of the other gollywoggles cries as he points into the trees to his left.

Rowan can hardly believe it. Several large half-rotten bears separate themselves from the trees and begin lumbering toward them. The gollywoggles group themselves behind

Rowan. Looking up at him, Slade tugs on his shirt, and asks, "Yer grace, what should we do?"

"It's just another one of Kieran's childish tricks. Nothing to concern yourselves with. Let's just keep moving." The gollywoggles bunch themselves around his legs. "Do not be alarmed. They are no match for me! Even though they are dead, they were risen by dark magic, and the magic knows that it will not stand against my power. They will eventually give up and go in search of other food. If you stay close and do not fall behind all will be well for you." Before continuing, Rowan places a guarded spell that will move through the ground with them. If anything comes within several feet of them he will know.

Keeping to the shadows, the dead bears follow, chunks of fur slipping from their bodies now and then, revealing sticky, slimy, gooey flesh. Their putrid stink permeates the air.

# A FEATHER, A SNEEZE; CHAOS IF YOU PLEASE

"And fight!" Are the last words he hears before the wolves attack! Sitting on top of Finn's shoulder all Bohdi has time to do is grab ahold of Finn's coat so he isn't thrown to the ground in the melee.

Asher swings his hammer, crushing the skulls of one wolf after another.

Finn slashes and stabs, cutting his way through the horde of wolves, lopping off heads as he goes.

The two brothers always keep their pets back to back. Arlo and Ryder crush the wolves in their jaws and throw them back into the forest when they get close to their masters. Bohdi desperately tries to hang on as Finn and Ryder twist and turn, buck and kick, and slash and chop at the wolves, but they just keep coming in a never-ending wave of teeth and slime.

Bohdi remembers his feather and what Asher told him. Reaching into his jacket he withdraws it only to have it knocked from his hand when a large wolf sails over their heads lunging for Asher. Finn reaches up and grabs ahold of its leg while swinging his sword in an arc and cuts off its head.

Bohdi drops to the ground in an attempt to retrieve his feather and finds himself in the middle of several wolves, their jaws snapping at him. Slime and goo fly in his face as the wolves advance, snapping and snarling. They lower their heads, and he can feel their hot breath as they wheeze in his face. They snap their jaws at him, bouncing on stiff legs, enjoying the game before killing him. Keeping his eyes on the wolves and trying very hard not to move, he searches the ground for his feather and finds it between his knees. With shaking hands he tries to pick it up. He has a hard time pinching the quill between his fingers and keeps losing it. "I sure hope Asher is right about this."

The wolves are on him now, drooling black ooze on the top of his head, their breath hot and stinking. Finally grasping the feather, he slowly inches it up between his knees. "Let it work. Please let it work." Bathed in slimy drool, he brushes his nose repeatedly with the tip of the feather, tickling and sniffing, tickling and sniffing several times. The battle between his brothers and the rest of the pack rings in his ears. Time for Bohdi has slowed, as the hot putrid stench of death surrounds him. Swishing the feather against his nose in earnest, he screams in his head, *Work, you blasted thing!* He sucks air in through his nostrils really hard, and the feather disappears up his nose and instantly—*Aw Chew!*—a colossal sneeze unlike any other erupts from Bohdi.

He opens his eyes and can hardly see anything through all the feathers floating around him. He can hear his brothers swishing their weapons through the air, stirring up the feathers. "I think you can stop now!" Bohdi calls out.

"What?" The two brothers stop. They look around, waving their arms through the air and trying to brush the feathers aside, looking for Bohdi.

"What happened to the wolves?" Finn asks.

Bohdi walks over to his brothers, smiling. "It worked is what happened! Asher was right. You should have seen me. I was terrified! There I was, sittin' on the ground surrounded by wolves, their drool dripping down onto the top of my head. Just when they were about to eat me, I find my feather, take a hearty sniff, suck the feather up my nose, and poof! A sneeze to beat all sneezes. I open my eyes and see nothin' but feathers floatin' all around."

Asher and Finn look at each other and smile as they hoot and holler, waving their arms through the cloud of feather. "Aw Bohdi, I knew we could count on that honker of yours. That beautiful wonderful honker," Finn says, reaching down and picking him up and patting him on his shoulder.

"Don't go get all gushy on me now."

They decide to circle back to the falls, nudging their pets they break into a run. Their voices can be heard regaling each other about their part in the fight, counting off how many wolves each killed and laughing about how it all turned out as they race through the forest.

The two yaksha step out of the shadows. They walk to the center of where the fight took place, swishing their feet through the feathers. The smaller yaksha bends down and picks one up. "The small one has great power." Its chilling breath misting the air.

"Yes, it would seem that there is more to these travelers than the king has told us." Again the chilling voice mists the air. "Do we follow or do we hunt? I am in need of food."

"We hunt first, and then we follow! There are plenty of goblins about. One or two will not be missed, and they scare easily," the taller one says, a thirsty gleam in his eyes.

"Agreed. Should we tell the king what we have seen?"

"No, our allegiance is not to him. Kieran is only paying us to track the girl. Any knowledge we gain is our own," he hisses.

The two glide off, blending back into the forest.

"I find all this waiting extremely boring, don't you, Zara?"

"It is tedious. I miss the storm we created; it was fun."

"I'm not looking forward to the battle, but I wish there was something we could do!"

Zara hears something crashing through the brush behind them. "Hide!"

The two tuck themselves behind a set of boulders and wait.

Crashing through a thicket of brambles the gollywoggles push and shove one another as they stumble onto the ledge of a cliff, cursing and calling each other names, creating quite the racket.

"Do any of you know how to be quiet?" Rowan asks.

Slasher looks up at the prince, a grumpy expression on his face. Pointing a long bony finger at him, he asks, "And just what do ye mean by that? We have been bein' quiet, talkin' in whispers! Why we've barely made any noise at all!"

Rowan looks down at the small troop of gollywoggles as they all bob their heads in agreement with Slasher. "Hopeless, you're all hopeless! Just keep your eyes open for anything suspicious, and stop with all the pushing and shoving and whispering!"

"Yer right grouchy for a prince, ain't ye!" Snorbert remarks. "I'm just sayin', a tad more kindness on yer part would be a welcome surprise!"

"Cuz ye have done nothin' but complain this whole trip! And here we be helpin' ye with yer troubles and all. Just sayin', yer highness!" Scallywag grouches as he crosses his skinny arms over his chest.

Rowan stares down at them, his left eyebrow cocked upward. Opening his mouth, he suddenly clamps it shut, turns around, and walks off.

The gollywoggles all look from one to another. "Well, that be a might rude!" Slade says as they take off after Rowan.

The rest of the gollywoggles make comments to the affirmative as they go. All except Kevin, who hasn't uttered a word as he falls into step behind all the others again. He seldom ever speaks, and no one ever pushes or shoves him or calls him any names. They all think he's crazy because he keeps to himself, listening and learning. Most of the time everyone forgets he's even there, and that's the way he likes it.

Up ahead Rowan is finally free of the trees he's been winding his way through and stands on a ledge overlooking a canyon. He can see Sadie some distance away on another ledge with Daghan and the others fighting off a hoard of undead squirrels. From his vantage point she seems to be having fun. She doesn't seem to be frightened at all. Pride swells in his chest as he watches her throwing bombs at them. Suddenly the wind starts to pick up and they all hunker down. *Raine,* he thinks to himself.

Stepping out from their hiding place Ezra and Zara follow Rowan and the gollywoggles, their packs full to brimming with all their concoctions. The heavy burdens make their trek awkward and slow.

Having watched Rowan pass within a few feet of her after all these years causes an unexpected tightness in Zara's chest, a longing. She had wanted to step out and greet him, talk to him. Unhappy about the unwanted stirrings she's been having, she shakes herself mentally and trudges on in silence.

Ezra, sensing something is troubling her friend, begins to wonder. What does she really know about her? Zara has never spoken to her about her past before they met. She's never said a word about her family or what realm she comes from. Thinking about it, Ezra realizes that she knows very little about her. Frowning, she asks, "Zara, what has been troubling you this night? You seem to be occupied elsewhere in your mind!"

Startled by the sudden questions, Zara answers, "I have been thinking about what may come this night. I admit, I am a bit unnerved." Hoping to derail her train of thought because she doesn't want to discuss her feelings, she continues, "Are you not the least bit concerned about how this night could end, for us I mean?"

"I've not really thought about it. I guess I've been more concerned about what will happen if our king doesn't get his way and win this battle or whatever it will turn out to be."

Stopping and turning toward, Ezra, Zara says, "Well, you should think about it—we need a plan! Our king certainly has not provided us with any helpful information. What if we are attacked? Do we use the potions we made for the king to protect ourselves? And then what? I truly feel we are in over our heads this time, Ezra, and I don't like it!"

"Since when have you become so thoughtful of mind? Tis unlike you, Zara. I can't help but feel that there is something you are keeping from me. Why have you never spoken of your past or where it is you come from?"

"What? Why do you bring this up now? To be honest, I never thought you were interested! Besides, I do not believe in living in the past; no future can be found there! That is why I do not talk about it, if you must know!"

"Hmm. I still think you're keeping something from me. But I guess you have a right to your own thoughts. I just don't want them to be a distraction tonight."

"Do not worry yourself with my thoughts! You should be worrying about surviving this night!"

Hearing the snap of twigs several feet away, Ezra raises her hand to silence Zara. They look around for a place to hide but see nothing but trees and bushes. Zara motions toward a fallen tree, and they squat behind it, waiting. They hear the thrashing and snapping of twigs getting closer. Whatever it is, it's moving at a very slow pace.

Ezra whispers, fear gripping her, "Do you think it could be a giant toad?"

Zara gulps. "I sure hope not! Listen! It doesn't sound like hopping. I've never heard that kind of sound before. It's more like something is being dragged, don't you think?"

"Well, they don't always have to hop, do they?" Ezra asks, terrified. "Maybe they're half walking, half dragging themselves?"

Zara throws her a disgusted look. "Just stop talking and listen! We need to do something! This tree doesn't hide us at all!"

They drop down and begin digging at the soft earth under the tree. As the sound grows louder, coming closer, they claw at the ground in earnest, scraping away large amounts of the soft soil. Panic drives them to dig faster.

Unexpectedly, the cloying perfume of rot and decay assaults them, and they gag in response. Pulling out armloads of the soft dirt, reaching farther and farther under the tree, they work at digging a space large enough to accommodate both of them. Fighting the bile that repeatedly fills the back of their throats, they toil at widening the trench they're digging to almost the full length of the fallen tree.

Branches and twigs snap, and the slow dragging sound is very close now, just beyond the tree. The putrefied smell of a rotting corpse hangs so thick in the air that the taste of it clogs the back of their throats. Flattening themselves against the ground they push in under the tree. That's when they hear the first *crack*.

Their heads snap around, their eyes wide as they face each other, horrified, fearful expressions on their faces. "Uh-oh."

Suddenly the tree's weight shifts, and they hear the *crack, snap, and pop* of its limbs breaking as one by one its branches give way and the entire tree pitches forward. Rolling onto their backs they grab hold of the tree.

Standing on the ledge where he had last seen the demoted ones, Kieran can't help but notice the foul smell permeating the air. With a thought he wraps himself in a barrier to block the noxious odor.

His assassin, standing beside him, asks, "My Lord, did you send those two lack-wits somewhere else?"

"No. I can only assume that whatever is causing this odor has scared them off. I'm sure I'll meet up with them somewhere. In the mean while I want you to go and round up the rest of the troop and meet me back at the clearing."

"As you wish, my lord." He silently disappears into the forest.

Kieran remains for a moment to look around. "Now which way did those two old crones go? Obviously something crashed through those brambles, forcing them to flee in that direction." He points upward toward the ridgeline.

Examining the trees and bushes more closely around the small ledge, he perceives a few broken limbs and numerous scuffs in the dirt. Feeling bored, he decides to follow the trail. While walking he searches the flora for continued signs of passage.

Completely engrossed in his search, the tall trees blocking most of the moonlight, he doesn't realize that he's wandered off the path, traveling down into the canyon instead of following the path upward and across. As he stops to assess his whereabouts he hears a high-pitched scream and then another. Looking around, he tries to ascertain which direction the screaming is coming from. Listening, he becomes conscious of the fact that something huge is rolling downhill. He swivels his head from side to side and listens as the constant wailing and screaming grows louder. As he looks up he catches a glimpse of a large tree rolling and bouncing its way down the mountainside heading straight for him.

Bursting into view, the tree flattens a thicket of crinkleberry bushes a few yards above him before hitting a large rock. It then bounces off the rock and is catapulted up into the air. He watches the tree soar over his head, two forms desperately trying to hang on with their hands as their bodies and packs fly free of the tree. Blood-curdling wails are torn from their throats as they sail through the air helplessly, spinning around the tree only to hit the ground with a resounding thud. The two stupidly continue to hang on to the tree as it bounces and rolls its way down the mountain, their bodies being first dragged and then wrapped around the tree as it ricochets off other trees and rocks, rolling through thorny bushes that tear at them as they go. Their screams ring clear and loud through the forest.

"Oh, there you are! I knew I'd find the two of you," Kieran says, chuckling. "How the two of you always manage to find yourselves in the most precarious situations is beyond my comprehension. However, you do provide excellent entertainment for me," he calls after them, laughing as he follows the trees trajectory. "I do hope their little trip down the mountainside does not destroy all the goodies they have made for me. That would be a troubling inconvenience!"

The tree finally slams into a couple of boulders resting close together, causing it to come to a sudden stop. The two exhausted fairies drop to the ground, their bodies shaking uncontrollably. As they work to calm themselves they scan their bodies mentally for broken bones or deep lacerations. What they find is that their pain is minimal. A few bruises and scrapes but nothing serious. Relieved, they start to laugh, first one and then the other until they are both laughing and crying hysterically. This goes on for some minutes before they stop and sit up to face each other.

"That was a terrifying ride!" Zara giggles, her eyes wide as she looks back up the mountain where they came from.

"I'm surprised that we are still alive!" Ezra smiles. "It baffles me that our bones are intact."

Standing, they look around for their packs and find them in a heap several feet away. They rush over to them and drop to the ground, and quickly digging through them to see what they might have lost.

"Most of my potions are gone! Smashed and broken, including my orbs!" Ezra cries.

"Several of mine are lost too. But I still have the orbs you gave me. I wrapped them more carefully than the rest," Zara replies, relief lacing her words.

Abandoning her pack, Ezra stands. She looks up, hearing a faint sound, and squints into the darkness. "Do you hear that? It sounds like someone's yelling."

Zara stands, slinging her pack over her shoulder and listening. "It does sound like yelling. Can you see where it is coming from?"

"No, tis too dark, but I can tell it's coming from somewhere up above. It sounds like the voice of a child."

"You don't think it is one of those nasty little imps playing a trick on us do you?" Zara asks.

"No, I don't believe so. We should climb higher up the canyon. Maybe then we can see who it is."

"Good idea." They turn and start walking, following the ridge of the canyon upward. "Ezra? Do you have any idea what was causing that horrible smell and the creepy dragging sound before we fell? Were you able get a look at it? I did not. I was too afraid to look."

"No, I was too busy digging." Looking sideways at Zara, she asks, "Did you hear a voice call out to us as we went flying through the air? I would swear that I heard the master call out to us. Isn't that odd?"

"I heard nothing but our own screams. I hope to never do that again. Although it did get us away from whatever it was that was following us and stinking up the forest!"

"True. I still can't believe that we didn't break any bones. Mayhap our luck is changing. Wouldn't that be nice?"

"It would be if we had any luck to begin with. We would have to have luck in the first place for it to change."

"Oh, don't be so negative. Luck is luck; whether it be bad or good tis still luck! I choose to believe ours is changing, so don't be such a sourpuss."

Zara gives Ezra a friendly shove. "Philosophical now? I think I like it."

As their path grows steeper they quiet down and concentrate on their footing, unaware that they are being watched.

# WHAT A RUCKUS

Asher, Finn, and Bohdi approach the edge of the canyon on the other side, intending to follow it up to the falls. The way they see it, they can only be attacked from one side this way. What they see is Ezra and Zara walking up the other side.

"Look! There on the other side. It's those two bam pot fairies. I wonder what they're up to," Asher says, reaching forward to give Arlo a good scratch behind his ear. The bear enjoys the feel of it for a minute and then shakes his massive head.

Looking farther up the canyon, up above Zara and Ezra, Finn sees Rowan and the gollywoggles standing on a ledge. The gollywoggles are jumping up and down, waving their arms in the air, except for one who's standing off to one side. Rowan is looking out across the canyon. Finn tries to follow Rowan's line of sight, but there are too many trees, boulders, and cliff ledges in the way for him to see what he's watching.

Pointing upward, Finn says, "Look, there's Rowan and those ridiculous gollywoggles. I doona know what they're doin', but Rowan seems to be watching someone or something on our side of the canyon. I've tried but I canna see what it is that he sees."

All three of them gaze upward. "If that blasted bird of yours wasna still mad at you, you could just fly on up there and see what all the ruckus is about," Asher says to Bohdi.

"Well, you best be rememberin' that it is your fault she's mad at me!"

"She can be mad all she wants! Facts are that it worked! We'd all be wolf chow or undead ourselves right about now if you hadna plucked those tail feathers and you know it!" Asher banters.

"Knowin' it and likin' it are two vera different things, Asher!"

Finn looks from Asher to Bohdi as they continue to argue. He turns Ryder and heads up the canyon. "Come on, Ryder. I am tired of listenin' to those two argue about those blasted tail feathers! We have more important worries to be frettin' about. Like what is happenin' at the top of this mountain." Ryder shakes his head in agreement as he leaps onto a boulder.


"Are you sure there isn't an easier way up this mountain, Daghan?" Baba puffs as she throws her leg over the ledge and pulls herself up and onto it with Papa's help. His hand is firmly placed on her bottom as he pushes her upward. Rolling on to her back she says, "I wonder where all those gross little zombie squirrels went. I could use a break about now."

Sadie giggles, "That was fun, huh, Baba."

"A lot more fun than climbing! Hey you're a magic fairy, why don't you just sprout some wings for Baba and fly me the rest of the way up. Be a good little fairy and do that for me will you?" she says playfully, lying on her back and still puffing a little.

"Sorry, Baba. I would if I knew how, but I haven't learned how to do that yet."

Daghan looks at Sadie and says, "You don't learn how to sprout wings, Sadie. You either have them or you don't. Besides, *you* are not that kind of fairy. You don't need wings. Once you're trained you'll be able to travel by thought. You're a royal."

"Did you hear that, Baba? Travel by thought! I won't need wings."

"First we need to get you home, munchkin," Papa says, hauling himself over the ledge.

"That's right!" Raine joins in as she floats down from somewhere up above. "Mom, it's just a little farther from here. A couple more ledges and we walk the rest of the way."

"Easy for you to say! Hey, how about you just whip up a floaty chair for me? If you loved me you would."

Laughing, Raine walks to her mother and squats down. She reaches a hand out to her, asking, "How about a hand up instead?"

Standing, Baba says, "I still think a floaty chair would be nice." Laughing, they all continue climbing.

Daghan finds himself amused by the female banter. He notices how comfortable Raine is around the humans. He realizes that she has grown to care deeply for them.


Reaching the crash site of the tree, Kieran looks around. He notices the pack laying on the ground and walks over to it, using the toe of his boot to push it around. Hearing only the sound of crunching glass, he leaves it. "What has gotten into those two?" He looks around for the other pack. "Hmm. Where would they have gone from here?"

Rowan senses Kieran first. He knows it's only a matter of time before Kieran senses him. Reaching out with his magic, he creates a spell for Kieran that will not only block him from transporting but will cause adverse reactions for him every time he uses magic. Satisfied, he groups the gollywoggles together and transports them all above Sadie and the others. There they wait for them to finish their climb.

Kieran walks to the edge of the canyon and looks up and sees Daghan and Sadie hanging from his back as he easily scales the cliff face. He thinks of transporting himself to their location. But instead of reappearing at their sides, he finds himself shrinking to half his original size. "What is happening?" he shrieks.

Searching for the reason behind what has happened to him he touches on Rowan. He can feel Rowan smirking. Anger expands in his chest, and he kicks at the ground, roaring in rage, and then suddenly starts to cough uncontrollably. Dropping to the ground on his hands and knees, he coughs out several moths. He sits back on his heels and bellows at the top of his lungs, "I will come for you Rowan, and when I do, I will kill you very slowly with my bare hands. I swear I will!" His voice sounds squeaky and small.

He looks to where Daghan hangs with Sadie on his back, and growling in frustration he squeals, "I will crush you like the spider you are, Daghan! Then I will warm your chilly little girlfriend!"

"Big words from such a tiny man, Kieran!" Daghan calls back.

"I am not his girlfriend, you lack-wit!" Raine shrieks at him.

Rowan looks over the edge and sees Kieran. Smiling to himself, he sends a swarm of flying insects after him. Watching from above, he hears Kieran scream in outrage as he takes off, running up the side of the mountain, sparks shooting from his fingers into the dense cloud of insects only to bounce back and shock him instead. Try as he might he can do nothing to stop the swirling mass from attacking.

"That ought to keep him busy for a while. I haven't had this much fun since I was a boy!" Rowan laughs.

"Busy for a good long time, yer highness," Slade agrees, looking down over the side.

With Kieran's curses being called out intermittently from below, Rowan and the gollywoggles begin helping Sadie, Baba, and Papa over the last ledge.

The last they all see of Kieran is him veering off into the woods as the swarm engulfs him, electricity arcing and sizzling throughout the dark cloud. His yelps echo off the trees.

As everyone turns from the ledge laughing, their long climb behind them, Baba finally feels like they just might make it. They all walk into the forest chatting and laughing, their worries put aside for the moment, their hearts lighter.

Sadie and Baba both reach up and scratch their heads, Sadie once again gets that tingling sensation at the nape of her neck. Looking around she sees the bright yellow eyes glowing in the distance, and for the first time she feels comforted by them.

"The falls are just a couple of treks from here. We should reach them in no time," Daghan says cheerfully.

All at once a loud sneeze erupts from the forest in front of them, *Aw Chew!* Immediately afterward the elf brothers appear, running down the hill, their pets nowhere to be seen, all three of them wearing dresses.


"Finally, we're at the top. Let's just sit for a minute and rest, Zara."

Plopping down onto the ground, breathless, Zara replies, "Yes, I agree. I am glad this night is cool. The air feels good up here. How do we get to the other side from here, Ezra?"

"There's a bridge up ahead just a little further. Once we cross the bridge it's only a couple more treks to the falls."

"Why are we heading to the falls, Ezra? Why are they heading to the falls?"

"I can't explain it. I just feel that's where we're supposed to go," she says, shrugging her shoulders.

As they watch the elves running toward them, their dresses hiked up, a soft yellow glow lights the forest behind them. The elves never slow. They just blast past them looking over their shoulders and yelling, "*Run!*"

As Sadie watches, a swarm of giant fireflies shoot from the trees heading straight for them. All of them turn and start running, heading away from the falls. Rowan catches up to Sadie, easily lifting her into his arms as he runs, a big smile on his face. "I haven't been out and about having this much fun since I was a boy," he tells her.

Being bounced up and down as he runs, she smiles back at him. "It is fun, isn't it?"

Daghan, running up alongside Asher, asks, "So, what happened?"

"Well, we were almost ta where we had last seen all of you when all of a sudden Bohdi sneezes. Our pets disappeared, we're all wearin' dresses, and the next thing we know, we're bein' chased by giant fireflies."

"Well, I guess it could have been worse!"

Seeing the ledge, they both run straight for it and jump.

They jump off the small ledge one by one and drop to the ground and scramble backward, pressing their backs against the wall, making themselves as small as possible. It doesn't take long before the fireflies buzz past overhead. Rowan and Sadie are the first to start laughing. As the others look at the three elves wearing dresses, one by one they start to laugh too. Soon they're all laughing and talking as the darkness fades into the soft light of morning.

Walking back the way they had run from, Sadie has a chance to talk with Finn. "What will happen to the fireflies now?"

"They'll return to their normal size once the spell wears off, just like everything else does." Finn replies.

"They sure are scarier when they're big!" Sadie says.

"Oh, I'll agree with you on that, lass."

"We fought off a whole bunch of zombie squirrels while you were gone," Sadie tells him.

"What's a zombeh?" Finn asks.

"You know, the undead. Ooooh," Sadie says in a creepy voice.

Finn looks at her, a smile on his face, and says. "Ah little one, you are a treasure."

"We had to fight off a huge pack of wolves. Zombeh wolves, as you would say."

"It's pronounced zombie."

"That's what I said, zombeh."

Sadie giggles. "Baba likes the way you and your brothers talk. She says you all have a Scottish brogue."

"Does she now? Well, I guess my brothers and I will just have ta regale her with some of our tales some time."

"She would love that. You know when we started out last night it was just Daghan, Baba, and me. Now look at all of us. We have six gollywoggles, three elves, two humans, and four fairies. That's counting me as a fairy and not a human," Sadie adds.

"Quite the troop, arena we now? I would say that a lot has happened in just one night."

"It's been scary at times, but for the most part I'm having the best night of my life!"

Finn reaches over and musses her hair. "You're a real trooper, Princess, a real trooper indeed."

Walking just a couple of steps behind them, Rowan listens to Sadie and Finn as they converse. He intends to stay close to her, positive that they haven't seen the last of Kieran or his minions. Knowing Kieran he's sure that there will be an ambush at some point before the day is over.

Having finally escaped the swarm of insects, Kieran trudges along. Still only three feet tall, half the height he normally is, he's still fuming with anger. Once again Rowan got the better of him. The fact that his powers are so much stronger than his own means he will always have the upper hand. Rowan will always sense his presence before Kieran senses him, giving him the upper hand and allowing him to cast his spells without him knowing. That's why he's unable to block them.

"One day, Rowan, one day," he seethes. "One day I will have my full powers back, and then you will rue the day you were born. That I promise myself!"

Out of nowhere Gothock wonders into his path, "Gothock!" he calls. "Where have you been? I have been summoning you half the night! Why have you not appeared to me?"

Gothock's beady black eyes assess him. His tongue flicks in and out several times. The familiar taste and smell of his master is in the air, but he doesn't recognize the small creature standing before him.

"Why are you looking at me like that, Gothock? Don't look at me and lick your lips! It is I, your master!"

Finally he realizes that Gothock might not recognize him in this small form. Changing his voice from a commanding tone, he croons softly, "Gothock it is I, your loving master. Come here, boy."

Gothock lumbers forward, continuing to taste the air. As soon as Kieran touches him he knows that he is his master. The familiar touch of Kieran's hand is a welcome feeling. As Gothock leans into his master's hand, Kieran relaxes. "That's right, boy. Now we must fly and we must hurry."

He climbs onto Gothock's back, and they trundle off to find a suitable clearing for Gothock to take off.

"The falls are absolutely breathtaking, Ezra! Their roar so loud, much louder than I would have guessed," Zara shouts.

Ezra smiles at her friend. At times she seems very young, expressing herself with a childlike wonder.

"Have you never seen a waterfall before, Zara?"

"Yes, but it was a long time ago. A lifetime ago," she says wistfully.

Ezra looks at her closely, wondering yet again about her past life. "Where shall we wait?" Looking around, she says, "We need a place with a clear view of the falls. I don't want anyone sneaking past us."

"There!" Zara points. "That set of boulders above the falls should do, as well as affording us some protection if we need it."

"Very good. Now I need to rest. I'm exhausted," Ezra shouts over her shoulder as she heads for the rocks.

Landing in the clearing, Kieran prepares himself for the coming onslaught of quips and rude remarks his minions will surely cast upon him. He dismounts Gothock as regally as possible. All eyes turn to him, and he watches as the wary smiles form their faces. The yaksha are the first to approach.

"Your Highness," the smaller of the two greets him and bows. No sign of mirth about him.

The taller one bows as well. "Your grace." Standing, he looks down on Kieran. He is now a good three and a half feet taller than he is. "I see you've experienced a misfortune, to put it mildly," he hisses, the air misting around them.

"That is an understatement!" Kieran hisses back.

Those around them who heard his response start laughing, repeating the word *understatement* and then laughing some more.

Kieran clenches his hands into fists at his side as his face reddens. Relieved that they don't know that his magic isn't working correctly, he yells, "Shut up, all of you! Before I shrink *you* down and feed you to Gothock! Except for you goblins of course. He is quite capable of swallowing you whole."

All eyes at that point focus on Gothock. He looks around, his tongue flicking in and out, the long strands of poisonous slime hanging halfway to the ground. The goblins take several steps back, fading into the meld.

The taller yaksha asks, "Where are we to go from here, your grace?"

"To the falls. Have any of you seen my assassin?"

"Here, my lord." He breaks apart from the rest of the troop, and the ones closest to him jump, obviously not realizing that he was there.

Kieran smiles, enjoying their unease. After this is all over he fully intends to show them just how funny he can be. "Aw, there you are. A word in private."

The assassin walks over and squats down so that he is at eye level with his king. Knowing Kieran's propensity for getting even with those that he feels have slighted him in some way he says, "My lord, I do not mean any disrespect—quite the contrary. I only wish to show respect by not looking down on you while we speak."

His king smiles. "You know me well, Cyan. I also know you, and I know you enjoy your job and would not want to be replaced."

"True. You are wise indeed. How may I be of service?"

After the conversation with his assassin, Kieran remounts Gothock and calls for everyone to follow.

# THE AWAKENING

"Zara, what do we have left in your pack? I like the way the sound of the falls is muffled here."

"I do too. Not having to yell is nice."

Pulling her pack onto her lap, she reaches in and pulls out its contents one piece at a time, setting them on the ground beside her. "We have one sleeping potion and one transformation potion." Holding it up, she inspects it. "I am still not sure this one will work in the manner it is intended to, so we must be cautious with this one."

"If you aren't sure it'll work, why did you make it?"

"To see *how* it will work. What better time to try an experiment?"

"True. Good idea."

"Now let's see. I have the orb you gave me and the amnesia potion. One sickness potion, one stinker potion. I do so enjoy the stinker potion." She giggles at a memory. "That one fella thought if he took off all his clothes he could walk away from the smell, remember, Ezra? He was very disappointed when he found that he was the stinky one and not his clothes." Laughing, she reaches back into her pack and feels around. Her fingers touch on something familiar, something long forgotten, and she closes her hand around her necklace. Feeling a prick of melancholy, she says, "And that is it, six potions left." She slips her necklace back into its hidden fold inside her pack.

"That's not a lot to work with, and all of our spare ingredients were lost or ruined with my pack."

"We have what we have, so we will just have to make do. We need to keep a look out every so often. I do not know if we will hear anyone approach from up here."

Standing up, Ezra peaks over the top of the rocks and scans the area below the falls on both sides. "Nothing." She sits back down.

"I wonder why our master has not contacted us," Ezra queries.

"I am quite sure he has more important matters to attend to than us," Zara replies.


Soaring through the air, Kieran feels an all-too-familiar tingling start to spread through his body. He smiles as he transforms back to his original height. "Nice." He flexes his arms and legs. Needing to test his magic, he looks from side to side, searching his troop for the perfect victim. His gaze lands on a particularly stupid ogre who thought his recent predicament was hilariously funny.

First the idea and then a few whispered words and the ogre's feet ignite. Kieran smiles.

Surprised, the ogre begins kicking his feet and starts to scream as he looks around in a panic. The fire slowly spreads up his legs, licking at his bare flesh. The pain is excruciating, and the ogre howls, slapping at his legs and desperately trying to put it out.

"Perfect, absolutely perfect!" Kieran snickers.

By now all eyes are on the ogre, watching in horror as the flames creep slowly up his torso. One by one they all realize who has caused this, and their eyes shift to Kieran. His wicked grin and the superior glint in his eyes are all the testament they need. All those who laughed at him gulp in response as they watch the flames slowly, very slowly, consume their comrade. Their master is methodically extending the ogre's execution, making him suffer all the more for his laughter and insolence.

The ogre's pet has flown away from the rest, dipping and weaving through the air as its master flails his arms, slapping at himself.

The assassin looks on, grateful that he is much smarter than most.

The yaksha fly to the other side, away from the flames, unconcerned and uninterested.

The ogre's whole body is now engulfed in flames. His screams of agony are pitiful as the flames stall at his neck. They lick at his face, blistering it. The flesh above the flames begins to bubble, his screams dying in his throat as the flames engulf his head, and he falls from his mount. A silent ball of fire plummets toward the ground, and his pet evaporates into nothingness. All is quiet for a moment.

Kieran looks back and forth at his minions flying alongside him on both sides. Most of their faces are like masks, frozen in time, absolute terror etched into them. *Good*, he thinks to himself.

Slowly he begins to laugh, a twisted maniacal sound. Leaning forward on Gothock, he urges him to fly faster as he calls out over his shoulder, laughing, "That was the most fun I have had in a very long time! I am looking forward to more of it!" His laughing rings out loudly as he outdistances his minions, leaving them to wonder about his meaning.


Peeking over the enormous rock again, Zara sees a large troop making their way up the mountainside. She turns quickly, her back sliding down the cool surface of the boulder as she slowly descends to a squatting position, her expression worried, with a sick feeling taking hold in the pit of her stomach.

Misreading the expression on Zara's face, Ezra asks, "What? What'd you see?"

But before Zara can answer they both feel the presence of their master enter their minds. He imprints his image on them, saying, "I am almost there. Do not do anything until I get there!" Then he is gone.

Relief washes over Zara, glad that he came and went so quickly. She has been having second thoughts about their master since he tortured them by slowly squeezing the air from their bodies.

Ezra jumps to her feet. She peeks over the boulder to see what Zara saw. "Their troop has grown. What are those small ones, goblins mayhap?" She looks down at Zara still squatting, her back pressed against the boulder. Ezra taps her on the top of her head. "Are you in there?"

Zara looks up at her, rubbing the top of her head. "Of course I am in here!" she grumps. Standing back up, she joins Ezra in peering down at the large troop approaching them. She reaches down with her hand and kneads her stomach, the sick feeling building. "Suddenly I am not feeling so well, Ezra. I believe I am going to be sick."

"What has gotten into you? You have been acting strange all night."

Zara pins her with a probing stare. "I do not want to die this day; do you?"

"What do you mean die? Our master will protect us!"

"Are you sure? Do you really believe we mean that much to him? Think about it! Think about how he treats us, Ezra!" she says, grasping her by the arms, her eyes pleading with her.

But Ezra doesn't want to think about it. She shakes her arms free and backs away from Zara, looking at her as though a fungus has suddenly spread all over her body. "Stop talking about our master like that!" she snaps. Hunching down slightly, she looks all around, an expression of mild concern on her face. "What if he's listening?" she hisses.

"So what if he is? He's tortured us for much less than this!" She walks away, crossing her arms over her chest and hugging herself as if she is suddenly cold.

"Tortured us? What are you going on about? Our master has never tortured us! Sure, on occasion he has felt the need to punish us."

"Punish us? What he does is not a punishment, Ezra! It is torture, pure and simple." Bewildered, she paces. "All this time we have hated our queen for punishing us," Zara whispers. She looks up at Ezra as she says, "But she has never once caused us horrible, agonizing pain! Has she? Furthermore, our queen does not enjoy punishing us, but *he* does! Or didn't you notice the last time!" Zara sneers.

"Who are you? What have you done with my friend? Surely someone has cast a spell on you." Ezra walks over to the potions where Zara left them in a neat little row. She bends over and scoops up the orb. "I'll hang on to this for now."

*Maybe?* Zara wonders to herself. "It is just that I cannot shake the sick feeling growing inside of me. It has been gnawing at me something fierce." Searching Ezra's face, she says, "Something very bad is going to happen. Very, very bad, Ezra. I can feel it and it frightens me!" Tears form in her eyes.

Ezra looks at her friend. Zara is the only one to stick by her side all these years. If she were to be truly honest with herself she would have to admit that she is more afraid of their master than she is loyal to him. Fear is a powerful tool when used to control others.

"Don't cry, Zara. All will be well; you'll see."

"No, Ezra. All will not be well when this is over. Of that I am sure." Zara walks over to her pack and retrieves it from the ground. Reaching inside it, she withdraws her necklace and slips it over her head. She presses the pendant against her chest as tears slide down her cheeks.

Rowan's head snaps up suddenly, and his thoughts scatter as he's overwhelmed by the feelings of sorrow and regret. *Zara*, he thinks to himself. The strong feelings of warning and worry for Sadie come to him. *I understand,* he whispers in his heart. Strong feelings of love and longing flow between them. Rowan has missed her for such a long time.

Rowan has everyone gather around him as he tells them that they are walking into an ambush.

"And just how have ye come by this information?" Slasher asks, always suspicious.

"Let me just say I know how Kieran's mind works and leave it at that, shall we!"

"What do you suggest we do?" Asher asks.

"We need a plan. I need to know exactly what everyone is capable of doing. Daghan, I know what you are capable of. How fast can you transform?"

"Fast! Almost instantly. Why?"

"Because I guarantee you that at some point you will need to."

"I can transport myself and at least two others invisibly if I need to. The downside to it is that it zaps all my strength and magic. I am left weak as a babe for a wee bit afterward," Asher explains.

"Good to know. We will save that to use only in an emergency. Finn, Bohdi, what about the two of you?"

"Ryder and I are a powerful force to be reckoned with. My swords can cut through anything, just like it's butter. Oh, and if I can catch someone unawares and tap them in the chest with one of them, it knocks them right out. They sleep like a babe for a good long while."

"Bohdi, what about you? Can you control your sneezing at all?"

"Well, I doona wish to get your hopes up, but I was able to take care of a whole pack of undead wolves last night," he brags. "Turned them all into feathers."

Rowan looks at the other two for reassurance. They both shrug their shoulders and nod their heads up and down.

"Okay, well. That does sound reassuring. Daghan, you and Raine will take the humans and Sadie to the falls. Asher, Finn, Bohdi, and I will keep Kieran and his minions off your trail. Slasher, I need you and your friends to spread out and keep watch over everyone. I want all of you to stay out of sight and report to me where Kieran and his followers are at all times."

Amulets appear around each of their necks. "These will keep all of you in constant contact with me. Lose your amulet and you are on your own, understand?"

Their heads all bob up and down in the affirmative—all except Kevin, who just stares at Rowan.

Bending down, Rowan whispers to Slasher, "Can that one understand me?"

"Aye! But it's like I told ye before—there's somethin' not quite right about that one," he whispers back. "Anyway, he understands well enough."

"Any questions?" He looks down at the gollywoggles.

"Why ye be lookin' at us?" Slasher grumps.

"You all spread out, stay hidden, and head for the top of the falls."

The gollywoggles take off in different directions and within minutes are nowhere to be seen.

"Daghan, throw out traps behind you as you go. That should slow down who ever will be put on your trail. Move as quickly as you can but as quietly as you can."

Sadie walks up to Rowan and wraps her arms around his waist, hugging him to her. Looking up at him she asks, "Will I ever see you again?"

Kneeling down, he wraps her in his strong arms and takes just a moment to savor the feel of her and breathe in her scent. He then kisses the top of her head and holds her out at arm's length. Looking into her periwinkle eyes, now shining with unshed tears, he says, "I will be at the falls before you slip through to go home; I promise. And I will come and visit you often in the human world once everything here is put to right, okay?" Brushing her tears away as they start to fall, he says, "I am quite sure that one day you will grow tired of me wanting to spend so much time with you. Now no more tears, for this is not good-bye but rather I will see you soon." He gives her another quick hug before standing and handing her off to Raine.

"Come on, munchkin. It's time to go."

Sadie runs to Finn and throws her arms around him, whispering, "I'm gonna miss you. Will you come and see me too?"

"I will indeed. You canna get rid of me that easy, Princess."

She then hugs Asher and Bohdi, saying her good-byes. Walking back to Raine, she says, "I'm ready now."

As they walk away a thick fog begins to roll across the ground, spreading up the mountainside and cloaking their troop in a thick mist.

Rowan turns to the elves and says, "When we get home, each of you will be rewarded handsomely for your efforts in this venture."

"The pleasure has been ours," Asher says, looking his prince square in the eye and smiling.

Rowan smiles back at him, and an understanding passes between them. "Yes, well, shall we go? I cannot wait to have some more fun with Kieran. Truly, I have felt exhilarated, like a young lad again. I think it has been good for me, all this excitement. I have been complacent for far too long. But not anymore. I have been enjoying this far too much to go back to the way I was."

The elves smile at their prince, understanding him completely and looking forward to what will come.

# SMALL PACKAGES, BIG IDEAS

"Raine, this fog is really cool. Is it so no one will be able to see us?"

"That's right, that and I knew you would like it."

"So, they can't see us, but we can see just fine?"

"Cool stuff, huh?"

"I'm just gonna be glad to get home. I'm really tired and I'm starving. It seems like we've been walking for days. I hope Mr. Frog is all right."

"I'm sure he's fine."

As they climb higher, the roar of the falls becomes louder; it's no longer a muffled rumble in the distance. Sadie gets that tingly feeling at the nape of her neck again and looks around for the giant wolf. "I can't see you, but I know you're out there. You don't scare me anymore."

"Who are you talking to, Sadie?" Daghan asks.

"I'm talking to the big wolf that saved me in the cave. I'm not afraid of him anymore, because now I understand that he's my friend."

"Really?" Baba asks. "Your friend? How do you know that?"

"I just feel it. He's been with me the whole time, Baba. I thought it was him that was calling to me in the forest when we started out."

"Someone was calling to you?" Daghan asks. "Why didn't you tell me?"

"I did tell you, remember? You came and got us from the bushes and I told you. I asked Baba a couple of times if she heard it, and she said no. So I just thought I was hearing things."

Daghan looks at her, one of his eyebrows raised, trying to remember.

Raine stops for a moment. "What did it sound like?"

"Well, it kinda whispered and it would call my name like 'Saaadieee.' Real creepy like."

"An imp!" Raine and Daghan say at the same time.

"Jinx, you owe me a Coke!" Raine tells Daghan.

"What? Jinx? What's a Coke? What are you talking about?"

Sadie giggles. "I guess he doesn't know that one."

Daghan stands there looking confused, not knowing what to say as Sadie and Baba brush past him and resume walking. Papa walks up and pats him on the back, saying, "Get used to it, son. In my world, men often walk around with that expression on their faces when dealing with women. I'm sure she'll explain it to you when she gets around to it." He walks off, a knowing grin on his face and catches up with the others, leaving Daghan to wonder what he was getting himself in to.

Kieran lands first at the top of the falls and dismounts, "Stay alert, Gothock. I don't trust Rowan! You get the chance to bite him, take it."

Gothock stares up at him, his beady eyes black as coal. His tongue flicks in and out, and he turns and slowly lumbers off.

As the rest of his troop starts showing up he notices that their numbers have shrunk considerably. Walking up to Kieran, the assassin says, "Your grace," and bows slightly. "As you can see, our numbers have dwindled. The show you put on for everyone sent them fleeing as soon as you were out of sight!"

"Did you make a mental account of who left?"

"Yes, your grace. We can hunt them down later at you convenience."

"Good. I do enjoy having something to look forward to. You know how I hate to be bored."

"Yes, your grace."

"Tell me, Cyan, do you think me overly cruel? Speak freely if you would."

"No, your grace." The answer came swiftly. "In my opinion you rule with a firm and just hand. Just as a king should."

"You're a good man, Cyan. I am honored by your loyalty and fidelity."

"As always, my liege." Cyan bows, an evil grin splitting his face. He secretly hopes that Kieran will perish in the coming attempt to abduct the queen's granddaughter. That way he can take his place as ruler of the dark kingdom.

"Now, let us go and retrieve my heir, shall we?"

"I look forward to it," he answers, his grin evil, his eyes sparkling with anticipation.

Both yaksha, two ogres, a troll, and four goblins approach, bringing Kieran's troop to a number of thirteen counting himself, the assassin, and the two demoted ones. The two separate troops of light and dark are now evenly matched in numbers. Thirteen and thirteen—those numbers alone should have been warning enough. In the fairy world the number thirteen is believed to be bad luck and is usually avoided at all costs. When large troops are necessary, their numbers either stop at twelve or continue on to at least fourteen if not more. On the rare occasion when humans are visiting Otherworld they are never counted as part of a troop when going into battle because they have no magic and they don't belong in the fairy realm. No human can kill a fae, but if they wield something made of iron they can injure them, making them weak.

As Daghan and the rest of them reach the bottom of the falls, an ogre and a couple of goblins step into the fog, blocking Sadie's path to the falls. Her eyes grow wide with fear as one of the goblins grabs for her. Screaming, she dodges its grasp and takes off, running blindly through the fog. Daghan curses and takes off after her, leaving Raine with the humans.

Running terrified through the forest, Sadie has no idea where she is running to. She only knows that she wants away from the awful, scary-looking thing that tried to grab her. Slowing, she gulps in air and stops and leans against a tree, trying to bring her breathing under control. Shaking all over, she squats down, her back pressed firmly against the tree, and puts her face in her hands and starts to cry.

*That was a stupid thing to do, Sadie!* She says to herself. *Now I don't know where I am, and no one else knows where I am either!* Realizing that crying won't help, she wipes her tears away and looks around. Standing, she looks around the tree. Nothing. *Just go back the way you came and everything will be okay*, she tells herself, trying to convince herself.

Stepping out from behind the tree, she starts walking quickly. She has only walked a few feet when a dark shadow steps out from behind a tree, blocking her path. She stops, sucking in a breath. Suddenly she hears a familiar voice behind her: "Here you are. I knew I would find you sooner or later."

Sadie whips around, coming face to face with Kieran. Backing up, she remembers the dark shadow and stops. "What, what do you want with me?"

"Do not be frightened, child. I have no intention of harming you, my sweet. I only want the chance to get to know you."

"Why do you want to know me? I'm nobody, just a kid like any other kid."

"Come now. I think we both know better than that. You are actually someone very special. You know it, and all of Otherworld knows it. Now, come along like a sweet little girl and there will be no need for anyone to get hurt."

"I'd rather eat bugs than go with you. I've heard all about you. My father says you used to be a royal stinker but now you're just a stinker!" She spits the words at him, showing much more bravado than she really feels.

"Why you impudent little—" He cuts his own words off, trying to get a handle on his anger.

"Takes one to know to know one, and it's not nice to call people names!"

"You just called me a name!"

"No, I didn't!"

"Yes, you most certainly did! Is your memory that short? You called me a stinker!"

"No, I did not!"

"Did too!" Kieran clenches his fists and stamps a foot at her.

The assassin stands there listening to the exchange of words and rolls his eyes.

"I did not! I said my father called you a stinker. Not me. Boy, you don't listen very well, do you?"

Kieran looks down at the young girl, a perplexed expression on his face. "You have guile, young lady. I will give you that. Now enough of this foolish banter! It is time to leave." Kieran reaches out to grasp her arm, but Sadie twists away and darts off through the trees.

Glancing over her shoulder, she turns back and almost runs into him. She backs up quickly to stay clear of his reach, clenches her small hands into fists at her sides, and glares up at him. "You'd better leave me alone or I'll—"

Kieran cuts her off. "Or you will what? Hmm! You are just a child. You are no match for me."

"I have powerful magic in me! My auntie says so! So you'd better watch out or I'll blast you with it! Bad things happen when I get mad. I'm warning you!"

Kieran and his assassin both start to laugh. "You are absolutely adorable, you know that? Quite the little imp! Go ahead—show me this magic. I would like to see an example of it, if you please." Placing his hands on his knees, he leans forward, staring at her, an evil glint in his eyes. "Well, I am waiting. Do it now!" he yells, startling her. Sadie backs up right into the arms of the assassin. She screams, and that's when Daghan drops down onto the assassin's back, knocking them all to the ground.

Sadie rolls away and jumps to her feet. Daghan is on his feet and has already transformed. In an instant he has grown much larger and has two sets of arms and glistening white fangs protruding from his mouth. He looks at Sadie and yells, "Run!" As he does so he feels the sting of a blade sink deep into his back. He whips around and comes face to face with an old adversary whom he thought long dead. The assassin smiles up at him. Light and dark fae face each other in the never-ending battle between good and evil, both capable of wielding unimaginable power.

Sadie runs as fast as she can, weaving in and out of the trees. As she runs past a crinkleberry bush, a large hand shoots out and grabs hold of her and yanks her into the bushes, clamping a hand over her mouth so she can't scream. Wide-eyed, she stares into the face of Slasher. He releases her and puts a finger to his mouth, silently telling her to be quiet. He then turns and peers through the bushes.

Daghan ignores the pain in his back. The assassin steps away from him and laughs. "Good to see you, my old friend. It's been a long time, yes?"

"You were dead!" Daghan says, his teeth clenched. "I sucked the life out of you myself!" he hisses, the pain in his back burning like fire..

"Yes, well, not completely. You left just enough life in me, making it possible for me to survive. Although I will say that it was pure agony fighting my way back to good health."

"I'll be sure not to make that mistake again!"

"I think you should know that my dagger has been laced with poison. I've been saving it for a special occasion; one just like this as a matter of fact. By now you should be feeling its slow burn. I had it made special just for you." He unconsciously reaches up to trace the scar under his eye with his index finger. "You see, I have long dreamed of this day. Of watching you die, writhing in agony as the poison burns its way through your body."

Suddenly Daghan lunges at him, grabbing him and lifting him off the ground. "Sorry to disappoint you!"

The assassin screams like an animal as Daghan sinks his fangs deep into his neck and drinks him in before tearing out his throat and ripping him in half just to be sure he's really dead this time. He flings the two halves away from himself, staggers, and drops to his knees. Before losing consciousness he summons Arabella.

Sadie and Slasher hear the scream echo through the forest, and then all goes quiet again. Wide-eyed, Sadie looks at Slasher and mouths, *What was that?*

"That be a death scream, lass," he whispers.

Kieran's boots suddenly appear directly in front of them. He's been popping in and out looking for Sadie.

"Sadie my dear, are you here?" He listens for any sounds. He can feel that she's near. "Come out, come out, wherever you are! I know you could not have gotten far. Oh, and by-the-by, my sweet, that scream you heard? I'm sorry to say that was your dear friend Daghan dying." He didn't really know that for certain but he couldn't pass up a chance to torment her.

Slasher looks at Sadie as tears well up in her eyes. He shakes his head from side to side, telling her that Kieran was lying. He then presses his hand over his amulet.

Unexpectedly Rowan is suddenly there standing before Kieran, startling him. "Rowan, what brings you to this neck of the woods?" Kieran asks as he glances around nervously.

"My daughter! Sadie, you can come out now."

Sadie and Slasher crawl from the cover of the bushes. She runs to Rowan in a panic. "Father, we heard a horrible scream; then *he* appeared." She spits the word *he* out like it caused a bad taste in her mouth. "He said that it came from Daghan when he died." Looking up at Rowan, tears form in her eyes again, and she buries her face in his abdomen, crying.

Anger overwhelms him, and he turns toward Kieran, but he's gone.

"He took his leave whilst ye were busy with the young lass, yer lordship," Slasher informs him.

"Good job, Slasher. We'd better get Sadie back to the others."

"No. I'm not leaving without Daghan. He saved me. If it wasn't for him Kieran would have kidnapped me. We have to go find him. Please!" she begs, looking up at him.

"Fine." Reaching out with his mind, he searches for Daghan and picks up on the faintest whisper of life. "I know where he is, but we must hurry."

Kieran materializes behind Ezra and Zara, "Where is it!" he hisses.

Startled, they both jump as they turn to face him.

"Where's what?" Ezra asks.

"The orb! You lack-wit! Where is the orb?" he screams at them.

Ezra runs to fetch it. Bending over she reaches for it only to be shoved out of the way by Kieran. Her face hits the dirt as he grabs the orb. Looking over at her, he sneers, "I didn't mean for you to touch it with your grimy fingers. I just wanted to know where it was."

As she wipes blood from her bottom lip with the back of her hand he disappears before her eyes, a disgusted look on his face.

Zara helps her to her feet, asking, "Are you okay?"

Ezra just turns and walks away without saying a word.

Rowan, Sadie, and Slasher arrive just as Arabella finishes cocooning Daghan. She stands over top of the cocoon, guarding him. As Daghan slips into a deep sleep inside the cocoon Arabella disappears.

Sadie lets out a small screech, clamping her hand over her mouth. She looks up at Rowan, "Does Arabella disappearing mean he's dead?"

Rowan squats down beside the cocoon and places his hand on it, concentrating. "No, he is still alive. We will take the cocoon with us. Raine will know what to do."

As they disappear Rowan looks around and notices the two halves of what used to be a man. He gathers Sadie to him, hoping she didn't see anything.

They all appear together just below the falls where Raine, Baba, and Papa have been waiting. Raine had already muffled the roar of the falls when they got there and decided to wait. Seeing the cocoon she jumps to her feet and leaps over Papa to get to Rowan's side. He gently lays the cocoon down on the ground.

Raine drops to the ground beside the cocoon and runs her hand across it. She looks up and says, "He's in a coma. Something very bad must have happened to him for Arabella to do this. He'll remain inside until he's healed."

"Will he be okay?" Sadie asks.

"Arabella wouldn't have cocooned him if he were going to die. She only does this after she bites him so he's protected while he heals." She gently rubs her hand across the cocoon.

"She bit him? Why?" Sadie asks alarmed.

"Her venom is poisonous to all except Daghan. For him, it's a healing elixir. I'm sure he will be just fine. I just don't know how long it will take."

Without warning Kieran pops in, grabs Sadie, and is gone before anyone can react. Rowan roars at the top of his lungs, bellowing his rage. He reaches out once again with his mind but feels nothing. Again he roars, and the air around everyone sizzles and snaps.

Kieran laughs at Sadie as she cowers against a tree, the orb gripped tightly in his hand. She eyes the shiny ball nervously. He holds it out to her, saying, "See this? I had it made especially for you. Was that not kind of me? Oh, do not be afraid. This will not hurt, or so I am told." He lifts the orb above his head intending to smash it against the tree above Sadie's head but is knocked to the ground by something big and furry.

"Oh, for the love of all things magic, what now?" he says as he picks himself up and looks toward Sadie.

Yamanu the huge timber wolf is there guarding Sadie. "Sure, now you show up! I have been trying to contact you all night! Where have you been, you mangy mongrel? I had a feeling you would turn out to be a mistake! I will deal with McWeenie when I get home. After all you were his idea."

As he takes a step forward, Yamanu drops his head, releasing a deep guttural growl. Drawing his lips back, he snarls and snaps at Kieran, spittle flying from his mouth.

"This cannot be happening to me! It simply cannot be happening! I must be dreaming." He wipes his hands over his face, drawing in a weary breath, and then throws his arms out wide and turns in a small circle. "Has the whole universes gone mad?' he shouts to the sky. "Is everyone and everything in it against me?" Sadie just stares at him. Crossing his arms over his chest, he reaches up to massage his chin with thumb and forefinger. "What to do, what to do?" He taps a finger against his chin and begins to toss the orb up into the air, playing with it.

Asher watches Kieran from behind a tree. He eyes the orb suspiciously. "Finn, go and tell Rowan where we are. I doona know what that thing is Kieran's tossing into the air, but I'll bet my boots it's nothing good for the lass."

Finn leaps onto Ryder's back and disappears against his fur. Ryder sprints away.

Bohdi shrinks and climbs up onto Asher's shoulder. "What do we do now?" he whispers in Asher's ear.

"We watch and stay ready."


Daghan bursts from the cocoon sucking in air loudly, filling both lungs. His abrupt entrance startles the troop, causing Baba to scream and jump away.

He sits for a moment gathering his wits and then looks around. It's not the first time he's burst out of a cocoon in front of people. The looks on their faces always amuse him. "What?"

Raine looks over at him and says, "Welcome back."

"What have I missed? Where's Sadie?"

Just then Ryder and Finn arrive. At first no one sees Finn. Then he moves, dismounting Ryder.

"Well, that's pretty cool," Baba says.

Finn winks at her.

"Well?" Rowan asks standing.

"Kieran has the young lass about a trek and a half from here. The huge wolf is with her, protecting her from Kieran. I doona understand everything he was saying, but apparently either Kieran or someone called McWeenie made the wolf from magic. It seems to have turned on Kieran. He calls it Yamanu."

"Let's go. Daghan you're with me. Raine, you take the humans and hide them behind the falls. Make sure all is ready to open the portal when we get back."

Rowan, Daghan, Finn, and Ryder disappear as fog swirls up, swallowing the others.

Raine, Papa, and Baba walk around the bodies of the ogre and goblins, Baba and Papa still amazed at how fast Raine killed them. Before they could blink she had an ice bough in her hands and shot all three of them, effectively freezing them solid instantly—quite the sight to behold.

Ezra and Zara find Kieran with Sadie and a giant wolf. "Master?" Zara asks, shaking him out of his revere.

"Aaah. Good you're here. You can help me with the unfortunate situation I have found myself in."

Ezra jumps at the chance to impress her master. Coming to stand next to him, she asks, "What can I do to help?"

Kieran quickly grabs hold of her. "You can play with the dog and keep him occupied for me," he says as he throws her into Yamanu.

At that point time seems to slow down for Sadie as everything happens at once. Yamanu grasps Ezra in his powerful jaws and begins shaking her like a ragdoll.

Kieran lifts his arm above his head to throw the orb at Sadie, but Zara jumps on him, grabbing his arm and struggling with him, buying Rowan the time he needs to transport himself to Sadie. Just as the orb sails through the air smashing against the tree Rowan wraps his body around Sadie, effectively shielding her from the parasites as they rain down on him instead.

Kieran knocks Zara to the ground, kicking her viciously. Then turns toward Rowan and Sadie, already whispering the spell he intends to use.

Out of nowhere Mr. Frog bursts from the trees riding a giant fire toad and waving a very small sword and yelling, "Attaaaack!"

More fire toads hop into sight, and Daghan remembers the acid in his pocket. An idea forms in his mind, and he whistles for Asher and yells for Rowan to get out of the way.

Daghan launches the bag of acid at Kieran as Asher swings his hammer into the belly of a fire toad, making it belch a stream of fire that ignites the acid just as Kieran turns to see what is happening. The flaming ball hits Kieran in the chest, setting him on fire as the acid works its magic, eating away his clothes and skin. He drops to the ground, rolling back and forth and screaming and writhing in agony as his flesh is consumed by the acid and flames. His skin bubbles and blisters before dissolving.

Suddenly Gothock comes running from the trees straight for his master as Kieran is managing to put out the last of the flames. Gothock runs straight to his master's side and lifts his leg, sprinkling Kieran with a steady stream, dousing the last of the flames as well as his master. Having done his good deed he trots off into the forest feeling very pleased with himself.

Everyone stares slack-jawed as the flames reignite, swiftly engulfing Kieran's head. He tries to scream, but the flames fill his lungs, sucking the air out of him. He starts grabbing handfuls of dirt and rubbing it all over his face and on his head. The flames die out quickly, but not before horribly disfiguring his handsome face and burning away over half his hair.

Kieran stands, shaking from the intense sickening pain that courses through his body. His clothes are half gone and hang from his body in tatters. His face and torso are badly burned and partially eaten by the acid. His beautiful hair is all but gone, and he is covered in dirt and drenched in the essence of Gothock. A guttural howl erupts from somewhere inside him, sounding more like an animal. Turning away from everyone he disappears, leaving his screams to echo throughout the woods.

A slow but steady laugh starts behind everyone. It quickly turns into a full-out belly laugh.

Everyone turns to see Kevin on his knees laughing uncontrollably. He's laughing so hard tears stream down his cheeks and he begins to hiccup. Finally, after several long minutes with everyone staring at him, their eyes wide with wonder because this is the first sound he's made, Kevin sits back on his heels and looks around. "What? Have ye never seen a bloke laugh before?"

# Epilogue

After the fight Mr. Frog magically disappears, called by the queen herself, as he tells the story later. She wanted to repay him for showing up at the last minute to help save the day. He says she offered him a kiss as payment. A kiss from the queen is a true treasure. With just one kiss the receiver is granted his heart's truest desire.

After kissing Mr. Frog, the queen stands back to watch what he will become, but nothing happens. Because his heart's truest desire is just to be himself, living his simple life as a big green frog on the lake that he loves with the new friends that he has made stopping by to spend some time with him.

The queen smiles at Mr. Frog, feeling humbled by such a gentle creature. He has given her a priceless gift in reminding her of how valuable the simplest things in life are and how often they are overlooked. Kneeling in front of Mr. Frog she plucks a single strand of golden hair from her lovely head and wraps it around his neck, whispering,

*"A gift for a gift,*
*My sweet little friend.*
*The student became teacher,*
*The teacher a friend."*

The golden strand of hair shimmers and becomes a golden chain with a single golden teardrop hanging from it. "A token given with love and gratitude is one of great power, my little green friend," The queen tells him. "I give it to you as proof to all that you are one of my most favored."

When Sadie arrives home she makes a beeline for the kitchen first, grabbing anything she can reach and stuffing it into her mouth and chugging milk from the bottle. Next she hits the shower and sits under the spray of water for a while after washing all the sweat and grime from her body. She leans back, enjoying the feel of the hot water, and breathes in the moist air. The familiar smell of lavender soap and baby shampoo surrounds her, making her feel safe and relaxed.

She crawls into bed and is asleep by the time her head hits the pillow. Twelve hours later she wakes feeling rested and happy. Stretching her legs, she feels something on the foot of her bed. She opens her eyes and sees Aunt Alece smiling at her. She blinks and says, "Good morning."

"Good morning, munchkin. I need to speak with you before you go downstairs." She pats Sadie's leg.

Sadie sits up, a little alarmed. "Did something bad happen while I was sleeping?"

"Oh no! No, nothing bad. I just need to tell you that our queen was here last night. Well, your grandmother, I guess I should say. Anyway, she decided that it was for the best if Baba and Papa didn't remember being in Otherworld. You need to understand that she has to protect the delicate balance between our worlds."

Tears swell in Sadie's eyes. "They won't remember anything? I won't be able to talk to them about the greatest adventure of my life? That hardly seems fair."

"I know, munchkin. I'm sorry that it has to be this way, but Baba still remembers Mr. Frog. A favor he asked of the queen." Sadie crawls into her arms and cries for just a couple of minutes thinking about it. Sniffing and wiping at her tears, she pulls away, "Well, at least I'll be able to talk to you about it, right?"

"Absolutely."

"Hey, don't forget about me," Daghan says, popping his head through the doorway.

"Daghan!" Sadie squeals in delight as she jumps from the bed and runs to him. "I forgot you were staying with us." She pulls him into the room. "But if Baba and Papa don't remember anything how are we gonna explain Daghan?"

"They think he's a friend of mine from college."

"Oh! Okay, I can keep a secret."

"I know you can." Alece reaches out and tweaks her nose. "Now let's get started on your training, shall we? The most important thing you need to remember is that magic is all about believing. Whatever you can imagine, if you can believe in it you can make it happen. You belong to an ancient line of royal fae, and you have the magic within you to create reality out of nothing with a single thought."

Later that week Sadie finds her backpack in the back of her closet. Opening it, she finds a gilded mirror. As she gazes at the image of herself the image giggles. "Hi Sadie. Don't tell Raine about this—it's forbidden."


Two years have gone by when Alece is awakened one night by a gentle hand shaking her shoulder. Opening her eyes she expects to see Sadie and is surprised to find Princess Serena standing by her bed, a frantic expression on her beautiful face.

"What has happened? Why are you here?" Alece asks, rubbing the sleep from her eyes.

"You must hurry. He needs you. Quickly—there is not much time. I have already spoken with Daghan and cast a spell to explain your absence. All will be well here until you return, but we must hurry!"

Whispering in hushed tones, Serena and Raine move farther away from the bed where Rowan lies magically bound. He struggles against his bonds when their backs are turned, always keeping a close eye on the two. His eyes glitter with hatred.

"You must do it now," Serena pleads. "I do not know how long the bonds I've placed on him will hold."

"I cannot!" Raine says, horrified by Serena's request. "What if you are wrong about him?"

"I am not wrong!" Serena hisses. "You must do this. It is the only way to save him! Listen to me. If you do not stab him in the heart soon the madness will take a stronger hold on him. It will continue to darken his soul until he is lost to us forever. Please! You must hurry!"

Walking to the edge of the bed, Raine stands by his side and gazes down at her friend. Looking deep into Rowan's eyes, she searches for something, anything that will tell her that all she has been told about him is true.

Glacial blue eyes stare back at her, pleading, "Do not do this. She is wrong. Look at me—I am well. I know you, and I know that you would not want me to die by your hand. Release me and all will be forgotten."

"Do not listen to him!" Serena snaps. "Do it! He is only stalling for more time to find a way to free himself. Do it now! I command you!"

Lifting her ice dagger above her head she hesitates. Rowan stares up at her and he begins to struggle, bucking and twisting, pulling against his bonds once more. "Do not do this!" he commands through clenched teeth. Hatred flashes in the depths of his eyes, but only for an instant, and then it's gone, replaced once again by his pleading stare.

"Do it! Do it now!" Serena shouts.

Convinced after what she saw in the depths of his eyes, she plunges her dagger deep into his chest, piercing his heart, and then withdraws it quickly.

His cry breaks the silence in the room, the sound more animal than man, more from hatred than pain. He roars, cursing them both at the top of his lungs, hatred glittering in the depths of his eyes as he struggles in earnest against his bonds.

The ice slowly spreads through his heart, his struggles slowing until finally they cease altogether as his eyes flutter closed. When he finally rests peacefully in a deep, deathlike slumber Serena and Raine gaze down upon the beautiful golden man. Pain and sorrow etched into their lovely faces, their tears flowing freely.

Serena looks up, squaring her shoulders, her head held high as she says, "Now your quest for the cure begins ..."

Here's a peek at my next book in the Sadie trilogy.

## Fungusamongus
### (A Fairy's Tale)

As Rowan lies in a deathlike slumber, Raine, Daghan, and Sadie embark on a dangerous quest that will take them to the farthest reaches of Otherworld in search of a cure.

They are told that the spores of a very rare and possibly extinct golden mushroom are said to be the cure to release Rowan from the dark madness that has taken over his mind and now sleeps within his body.

Princess Serena has provided them with a map and sacks full of golden magic runes. The map reads like a scavenger hunt, taking them through one portal after another and forcing them to travel great distances through unknown realms of strange fae, weird creatures, and at times forbidden magic.

Travel with them as they are joined by Asher, Finn, and Bohdi once more.

"The map says that the first portal is in the Cave of Dark Dreams," Raine says, blinking and hoping that she is reading it wrong.

"We have to go in there again? Is there an alternate route?" Sadie asks, hopeful.

"No, I'm afraid not. The Cave of Dark Dreams is the only way."

"Well, there's no sense in snivelin' about it if it canna be helped! We best be off. It'll be gettin' dark soon," Asher says, climbing onto Arlo's back.

"Right behind you, Asher. I'll be lettin' you lead the way into that cave!" Finn chuckles as he swings up onto Ryder's back.

Having called their pets, they each mount up. Sadie reaches forward and scratches Yamanu behind the ear. "At least this trip will be easier, as we know a little of what to expect."

"Expect nothin' the likes of what ye saw the last time, lass. As I told ye before, the cave changes along with all the things that slither through it!" Slasher exclaims.